# WITCH WARS

## SIBÉAL POUNDER

Illustrated by
Laura Ellen
Anderson

BLOOMSBURY
LONDON  OXFORD  NEW YORK  NEW DELHI  SYDNEY

Bloomsbury Publishing, London, Oxford, New York, New Delhi and Sydney

First published in Great Britain in March 2015 by Bloomsbury Publishing Plc
50 Bedford Square, London WC1B 3DP

www.bloomsbury.com

Bloomsbury is a registered trademark of Bloomsbury Publishing Plc

Text copyright © Sibéal Pounder 2015
Illustrations copyright © Laura Ellen Anderson 2015

The moral rights of the author and illustrator have been asserted

A CIP catalogue record for this book is available from the British Library

ISBN 978 1 4088 5265 1

Typeset by Hewer Text UK Ltd, Edinburgh
Printed and bound in Great Britain by CPI Group (UK) Ltd, Croydon CR0 4YY

14

*For Emlyn and Sinéad – S.P.*
*For Marie – L.E.A.*

# Prologue

For as long as anyone can remember, witches have lurked on this planet. They have brewed gloopy potions in their cauldrons and torn through the sky on their brooms. They have cackled. They have cursed. They have cats.

Most people think witches are really evil, with their tattered black dresses, pointy hats and unfortunate noses, but that's mostly nonsense and really only half the story. The truth, if you happen to be looking for it, lies deep down below the sink pipes ...

 1

# Down the Plughole

It would have been very difficult to spot Fran the fairy on the day this story begins. Her dress may have been puffy, her hair may have been huge, but she was barely the size of a small potato.

Fran was slowly sidestepping across a garden lawn, holding a large, limp leaf in front of her. She didn't want the owner of the garden to see her because Miss Heks was a terrible old woman with a grim face and size eleven shoes. If she had seen Fran she would've squashed her immediately.

Fran and her leaf were on a mission. There was something very important in the shed at the bottom of Miss Heks's garden. That something was a girl called Tiga Whicabim.

'You!' Tiga said, pointing at a slug that was sliding its way across an old stone sink. 'You will be the star of my show! You will play the role of Beryl, an ambitious dancer with severe hiccups.'

Tiga had been in the shed for hours. The evil Miss Heks had been her guardian for as long as Tiga could remember and she had quickly learned to keep out of her way. If she didn't, the old bat would make her sew up the holes in her disgusting, scratchy dresses. Or she would force Tiga to run up and down the garden in her gigantic, ugly shoes, bellowing things like 'FASTER!' and 'OH, DID YOU TRIP?' from the kitchen window.

Tiga shone a torch on the slug.

'You are going to be the best actor the world has ever seen!' she cried.

Fran sighed when she saw that.

Not because she'd finally found Tiga, after a long and perilous journey that had almost ended with her being eaten by a dog.

No, the reason Fran sighed was because she loved a bit of acting!

Despite her small size, Fran was a big deal in the world of show business. Everyone called her Fran the Fabulous Fairy (a name she had made up for herself). She had hosted many award-winning TV shows like *Cooking for Tiny People* and *The Squashed and the Swatted* and she'd played the lead role in *Glittery Sue* – a tragic drama about a small lady called Sue who got some glitter in her hair and couldn't get it out again.

'An actor you say!' Fran said, making Tiga jump.

Tiga stared, mouth open, at the small person that marched across the shed and – very ungracefully, and with much grunting – climbed up the leg of her trusty old rocking chair.

Fran stretched out a hand.

'Very delighted to meet you, Tiga! Now, it's pronounced *Teega*, isn't it? That's what I thought! I'm very good at names and absolutely everything else. I'm Fran the Fabulous Fairy. But you can call me Fran. Or Fabulous. BUT NEVER JUST FAIRY. I hate that.'

Tiga, understandably, assumed she had gone mad. Or at the very least fallen asleep.

She squinted at the little thing with big hair and then looked to the slug for reassurance, but it was sliding its way across the floor as if it knew exactly who Fran was, and was trying to escape.

'I don't think,' Fran said, pointing at the slug, 'that she should be acting in the lead role. She is slimy and not paying much attention.'

Fran wiggled a foot and a beehive of hair just like her own appeared on top of the slug's head.

'Much, much, *much* better,' she said.

Tiga panicked – the slug had *hair*! Not any old hair, a beehive of perfectly groomed hair! It was a split-second reaction, but with a flick of her hand she batted the fairy clean off the rocking chair.

Fran wobbled from left to right and tried to steady herself.

'Did you just *swat* me?' she snapped. 'The ultimate insult!'

Tiga tried to avoid eye contact and instead looked at

6

the slug. She couldn't be sure, but it looked a lot like it was shaking its head at her.

'WITCHES ARE NOT ALLOWED TO SWAT FAIRIES. IT IS THE LAW,' Fran ranted.

'I'm sorry!' Tiga cried. 'I didn't think you were real – I thought you were just my imagination! You don't need to call me a witch.'

'Yes I do,' said Fran, floating in front of Tiga with her hands on her hips. 'Because you are one.'

'I am one what?' Tiga asked.

'One witch,' said Fran as she twirled in the air, got her puffy dress caught in her wings and crash-landed on the floor.

'BRAAAAT!' came a bellow from across the garden. 'Time to leave the shed. Your dinner is ready!'

Tiga glanced nervously out of the window. 'If you are real, although I'm still not convinced you are, you'd better leave now. Miss Heks is a terrible old woman and she will do horrible, nasty, ear-pinching things to you.'

Fran ignored her and went back to twirling in the air. 'What are you having for dinner?'

7

'Cheese water,' Tiga said with a sigh. 'It's only ever cheese water.'

Fran thought about this for a moment. 'And how do you make this cheese water?'

'You find a bit of mouldy old cheese and you put it in some boiling water,' said Tiga, looking ill.

Fran swooped down lower and landed on the sink. 'Well, I'm afraid we don't have cheese water in Ritzy City – it's mostly cakes.'

Tiga stared at the fairy. 'Ritzy where?'

'*Riiiitzzzzzy Ciiiiity!*' Fran cheered, waving her hands in the air.

Tiga shrugged. 'Never heard of it.'

'But you're a witch,' said Fran.

'I am not a witch!' Tiga cried.

'You SO are!'

'I am not!'

'Definitely are,' said Fran, nodding her head. 'Even your name says so.'

And with that she flicked her tiny finger, sending a burst of glittery dust sailing across the room.

8

*TIGA WHICABIM*, the dust read.

Then it began to wobble and rearrange itself into something new.

*I AM A BIG WITCH.*

'You've cheated somehow,' Tiga mumbled, moving the dust letters about in the air. Most people would've believed Fran by this point, but Tiga wasn't used to magic and fun and insane fairies. So, despite this very convincing evidence that she might just be a witch, Tiga still walked towards the door. Towards the cheese water.

'TIGA!' bellowed Miss Heks. 'YOUR CHEESE WATER HAS REACHED BOILING POINT.'

'Cheese water,' Fran chuckled. 'Wait! Where are you going, Tiga?'

'To eat dinner,' said Tiga. 'Bye, Fabulous Fairy Fran. It was lovely to meet you.'

Fran raised a hand in the air. 'Wait! *What?* You're not coming with me to Ritzy City, a place of wonder and absolutely no cheese?'

Tiga paused. Even if it was a mad dream, it was better than cheese water. She turned on her heel and walked back towards Fran.

Fran squealed and squeaked and did somersaults in the air.

'WHAT'S GOING ON IN THERE? I KNOW YOU CAN HEAR ME, YOU LITTLE MAGGOT!' Miss Heks shouted.

Tiga could see Miss Heks stomping her way towards the shed.

'Quick!' Fran cried. 'We must go to Ritzy City right now!'

'*How?*' Tiga cried, frantically looking around the shed for an escape route.

'Down the sink pipes, of course,' Fran said as she shot through the air and straight down the plughole.

'Come on, Tiga!' her shrill little voice echoed from somewhere inside the sink.

Tiga leaned over the stone sink and stared down the plughole.

There was nothing down there. No light. And certainly no city, that was for sure.

The door to the shed flew open and splinters of old wood went soaring through the air.

'WHAT IS GOING ON?' Miss Heks bellowed.

'NOW!' Fran yelled.

Tiga wiggled a finger in the plughole.

*This is nonsense*, she thought, just as she disappeared.

# Ritzy City

Tiga slid down the pipe at a slug's pace.

It was not magical.

She had imagined if anything was going to happen it would be slick – something with a little *whoosh*. Instead it was more of a *smoosh*. With her cheeks squashed against the sides of the pipe, she squeaked her way very slowly to somewhere else. That somewhere else was Ritzy City, because although Fran may have been a bit mad she was no liar.

Tiga slipped out of the pipe, fell through a layer of thick black clouds and let out a yelp as she landed with a thud on the roof of a small market stall.

'An impressive landing!' Fran shouted as Tiga peeled her face off the soft canvas roofing. 'NO BROKEN

BONES OR DEATH! WELL DONE.'

Tiga blinked as her eyes shifted from the fairy flying in front of her face to what lay beyond.

For as far as she could see, everything was black and grey. There wasn't a drop of colour in the place. Even Fran's dress had changed from purple to a deep dark grey. But it wasn't all black and grey in a horrible way, like the shed at night. It was beautiful. Black fluffy clouds with soft grey edges hung in the sky. The pavements were lined with smart black market stalls that stretched as far as Tiga could see. Behind the stalls towered buildings built in shiny black stone that went up and up and disappeared into the clouds. From those clouds came trickles of water. But it wasn't rain. Tiga imagined it might be what rain looked like if someone forgot to turn it off properly.

She jumped down off the stall roof and peered out from behind it.

Further down the road, huge black vases held delicate grey flowers and little pruned shrubs sat proudly outside the gleaming black doors of townhouses

13

trimmed with black polished railings. And all along the street women marched about in the most magnificent dresses of every possible shape and fabric – silk, chiffon, velvet, long, short, puffy. And every woman in every dress wore the same wide-brimmed black hat.

Tiga just stood there with a huge, dozy grin slapped on her face. Ritzy City was the most incredible city she had ever seen.

'Oh dear,' said Fran as a woman pushing a sparkly black cannon pulled up next to them. 'Tiga ... you might just want to cover your ear–'

'NEWS FLASH!' the woman bellowed as the cannon spun to face the sky and ...

*BANG!*

Tiga dived to the ground.

When she looked up, hundreds of bits of paper were slowly floating back down to earth.

 15

'Is that … ?' she began.

'It's the *Ritzy City Post*, our daily newspaper,' Fran said as a copy landed on Tiga's head.

*WITCH WARS BEGINS TOMORROW* was stamped on the front page.

Tiga raised the paper in the air. 'What's Witch Wars? Where exactly are we? And why is that woman allowed to wander around town firing a *cannon*?'

Fran opened her mouth to answer, but the witch manning the stall on which Tiga had fallen interrupted them.

'Hello, I'm Mavis. Jam?'

Tiga shyly shook her head.

'But witches love jam,' said Fran. 'They can't get enough of it.'

'That's why all these stalls sell jam,' said Mavis. 'Apart from that one at the end. It sells cats *and* jam.'

Tiga got to her feet and dusted herself off. 'I'm not a witch, Fran. I don't care if my name says so.'

'Everyone's a witch!' said Mavis, organising her jam jars in a neat row. 'Well, everyone here at least.'

Tiga watched the women striding past her. They didn't look anything like witches.

'The hats are wrong for a start,' she thought aloud. 'Why aren't they pointy? The tops are completely flat and not witch-like at all.'

'Ah ha!' said Fran, twirling in the air. 'That means you've only seen a witch up there above the pipes in *your* world. When a witch travels up there, although frog knows why they'd want to, they're sucked up the pipes, you see. It destroys the hat, making it all pointy. And some witches get horrible warts on their faces from all the grime – it depends on the condition of the pipe they travel in. Some knock their noses and it makes them crooked. Their dresses become all torn and tattered. Pipe travel is a horrible business.'

Mavis handed Tiga a tissue. 'You've not done too badly, only a bit of slime on your cheeks.'

Tiga grabbed the tissue and started madly rubbing her face.

'I thought you were going to be one of those ones whose nose goes all warty,' Fran chuckled.

'What about the water?' Tiga asked. 'It's not rain, is it?'

'No,' said Fran, watching trickles fall from the dark clouds. 'It comes from houses where you'll find a witch, up there in the world above the pipes. Some of them don't even know they're witches,' she added, with an eyebrow raised.

Tiga sighed. It was becoming very clear that there was no arguing with Fran.

'Right, we'd best be off or we'll be late,' Fran said, clicking her fingers in Tiga's face. And with that they waved goodbye to Mavis and her jam, and made their way along the bustling city street.

'So this is Ritzy Avenue,' Fran explained, while perched on Tiga's shoulder. 'It's the main shopping street. Over here we have Cakes, Pies and That's About It Really, the baker's. They make beautiful cakes and pies and That's It Really, which is a special type of tart only available in Ritzy City. *Very* delicious.'

Tiga pressed her hands up against the window and stared open-mouthed at the cakes, but just beyond

them, further into the shop, was a very peculiar scene. Inside, all the witches were staring, open-mouthed, back at her.

'Oh, and over there,' Fran said with a squeak of excitement as she pulled on Tiga's hair, 'is Brew's designer clothes shop. I love it! They make special dresses for me because I'm quite fabulous and famous, and also abnormally small. Mrs Brew is Ritzy City's best fashion designer, but you almost never see her. She spends most of her time in that studio up there.' Fran nodded towards a large round window at the very top of Brew's.

Tiga was almost certain she saw the shadow of some-one walk past it. Then a chattering line of ladies burst out of the door and trotted down the street carrying black bags stamped with a huge swirly 'B'.

'Cool,' Tiga said, heading towards the door.

'No time for clothes shopping!' Fran said, zooming on ahead. Tiga reluctantly scuttled after her. She didn't want to lose the only person she knew in Ritzy City.

Fran screeched to a halt outside the most beautiful

townhouse Tiga had ever seen. And she had seen three townhouses.

'This is Linden House,' said Fran.

Tiga felt small and insignificant next to the huge building. On it there was a gigantic sign covered in lights that read WITCH WARS, and below it hung nine huge flags. On them were nine huge faces. Tiga didn't recognise any of them, apart from the last one.

It was her.

# 3

# Peggy Pigwiggle

'I knew they would use that photo!' came a voice from behind Tiga. 'It was taken years ago at school, and I'd forgotten to brush my hair. And my teeth. And that bit of cabbage was really stuck in there, you know, *really* stuck. And when I walked into that bee on my way to the photographer I just knew my eyelid was going to swell up like that. My mum swears there isn't a single photo of me looking normal and not injured!'

Tiga spun round and stared at the girl standing behind her. She had one of those wide-brimmed hats in her hand. Her black hair, although not as messy as in the picture on the flag, was wildly frizzy and covered in black gunk.

The girl stretched out a hand. 'I'm Peggy Pigwiggle. I like your mad clothes – you must be from above the pipes.'

'I'm Tiga,' Tiga mumbled, looking down at the not-at-all-mad jeans and plain T-shirt she was wearing. A huge glob of gunk fell from Peggy's head.

'Oh, don't worry!' Peggy said, looking from the gunk to Tiga's scrunched-up face. 'My hair isn't melting or anything. I tried … well, I tried to brew a potion to make my hair less frizzy, but there isn't actually a recipe for that …' She paused. 'So instead I tried one I found for taming bears.'

'Because your hair is crazy like a bear?' Tiga guessed.

Peggy nodded. 'And bear rhymes with hair.'

'Ah,' said Tiga.

And then there was silence.

And a bit more silence.

Tiga shuffled awkwardly from foot to foot and Peggy whistled a bit.

'Um …' said Tiga, 'how do you make a potion?'

Peggy's eyes widened. 'You don't know how to make a potion? Oh, frogfaces, this isn't good. I mean, I thought *I* was in trouble because I'm terrible at potions and rubbish at spells. Can you do spells?'

'No,' Tiga said.

'No!' Peggy cried. 'Oh, for the love of a frog in a hat, I don't know what to say! You're going to be in a lot of trouble tomorrow.'

The wind, it seemed, suddenly picked up and Tiga's flag, along with the eight others, began to whip about madly in the air.

'What happens tomorrow?' Tiga asked.

23

'Oh no you don't, Peggy Pigwiggle!' Fran said, clapping her hands as she raced towards them. 'Not too much friendly chatter – you'll be enemies tomorrow. ENEMIES!'

'What?' Tiga said. She looked at Peggy, who had a gunky eyebrow raised.

'We're here for Witch Wars, Tiga,' Peggy said. 'Didn't you know that? Why did you think your face was on a *flag*?'

Tiga stared up at the flags and shrugged. 'Mistake at the flag factory?'

'No, no,' Fran said with a smile. 'Tomorrow you fight! And the witch who wins, wins *everything*.'

'The winner of Witch Wars becomes Top Witch and gets to rule over Ritzy City and all that lies beyond,' Peggy said, all chirpy and relaxed. 'All you have to do is defeat every one of those witches on the flags up there, including me. But you will probably beat me, even without spells and potions, because I'm pretty dreadful at everything! You might not beat any of the others, though, if I'm being completely honest.'

In that moment Tiga felt everything spin around her. It was mostly panic, but also the wind a little bit. And Fran, who had lost control of her wings, was spinning round her head.

Tiga stared up at the faces on the flags. They all looked like normal girls, apart from one. She stepped closer to the rippling flag and peered into the dark soulless eyes of the terrifying witch printed on it. It was a face she decided she would be happy never to see again. She closed her eyes, took a deep breath and pinched her arm as hard as she could.

She'd had enough of Ritzy City. It was time to wake up.

# The Witch from that Flag

In the distance, high up on the mountain that towered over Ritzy City, two figures tore through the air.

Well, one did.

Felicity Bat was levitating.

The other witch, Aggie Hoof, was about three metres below her, perched on a cushion on the back of another witch, who was crawling down the road at an un-human pace, her arms and legs moving madly in circles like the wheels of a car.

'According to *Toad* it's not cool to have pointy shoes this week, but it might be again next week. And so WE MUST THROW OUT ALL OUR POINTY SHOES RIGHT NOW!' Aggie Hoof screamed.

Felicity Bat sighed. 'That magazine is stupid.'

'Oh no, Fel-Fel, it's fantastic. How else would I know if I was wearing the right thing? No one wants to be wrong when it comes to something as important as the shape of the very tip of your shoe.'

Felicity Bat didn't even bother to answer. She just rolled her eyes, lifted her finger and sent a spray of little beetles shooting into the air. They floated about, bashing into each other for a bit.

'NOT THE BEETLES!' Aggie Hoof squealed, covering her head with her *Toad* magazine.

'Quiet,' Felicity Bat snapped, raising her finger in the air again and zapping the beetles. At first they froze, and then little trickles of gunge started to ooze out of them.

Aggie Hoof wiggled about. 'Bleurgh! GUTS!'

The guts swirled around in the sky, then moulded into an arrow, which pointed directly at Ritzy City.

'PERFECT,' Felicity Bat said, as the dead beetles dropped on to Aggie Hoof's head.

Aggie Hoof scowled.

'Almost there,' Felicity Bat said, speeding up.

'We're going to win Witch Wars! WE'RE GOING TO WIN WITCH WARS!' yelled Aggie Hoof, who was very good at yelling but not so good at common sense. The fact that there could only be *one* winner in Witch Wars hadn't really occurred to her.

'*Sure*,' Felicity Bat said with a twisted grin. 'We'll win. You *and* me …'

'You were made to win this, Fel-Fel!' Aggie Hoof said.

'Yeah,' Felicity Bat smirked. 'If Granny Crayfish taught me anything, it's that you've got to be bad to win Witch Wars.'

'But wasn't the last Top Witch really nice?' Aggie Hoof asked.

'Those days are over,' Felicity Bat said with an actual witch cackle. 'It's about time someone brought some bad back to Ritzy City.'

# 5

# Pinching Never Works

Tiga was still pinching her arm as Fran ushered her into Linden House with Peggy.

'It's not real. You're in a shed, with a slug, and you've probably just hit your head. You're in a shed; you've hit your head. Slugs ...' Tiga mumbled, her eyes squeezed shut.

When she opened one of them, she didn't see the shed or Miss Heks, just Fran looking confused.

'You're really weird,' said Fran, staring at Tiga.

Tiga stopped pinching her arm and looked around the vast hallway in which she was standing.

Linden House reminded her of a hotel. A hotel that had eaten a really nice furniture shop.

'It's the grandest residence in all of Ritzy City,' Fran said grandly.

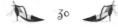

A marble staircase snaked up and up what seemed like about one hundred floors, but it was probably only about eight.

'Wheeeeeeee!' Peggy cried, racing through the door and into a room that was completely empty, but for a flowery, lopsided sofa.

'Careful, Peggy!' Fran cried as she zoomed after her.

Peggy spun around the room, splattering hair gunk everywhere, and then plonked herself down on the sofa.

Tiga giggled as Peggy bounced up and down, waving her arms in the air. But she soon stopped giggling when the sofa flipped round and disappeared through the floor.

When it flipped back again, Peggy wasn't sitting on it.

'She's a walking disaster, that one,' Fran groaned, soaring over to the sofa. 'Climb on, Tiga.'

Tiga walked slowly towards the sofa, eyeing it suspiciously. She put one hand on it. Then another.

'Oh, we don't have all day!' Fran shouted, pushing Tiga into the seat.

Unlike the room from which they'd just spun, the room into which they now spun couldn't have been more cluttered. There were stacks of chairs and books and at least five tables, and every inch of wall was covered in a painting of a beautiful map. Tiga walked slowly towards it.

'Cool, huh?' Peggy said.

'Is this … ?' Tiga began.

Peggy nodded. 'All of Ritzy City and beyond.'

'What *is* it?' Tiga whispered.

Peggy grinned. 'The land of Sinkville, of course.'

Tiga's eyes scanned the map, from Ritzy City to some docks, to hundreds of long spindly towers perched on a hilltop, all the way down to a tiny cluster of weird underwater buildings that were painted so close to the bottom of the wall she had to crouch down on the floor to see them.

'That bit,' Peggy said, slapping an area of the map close to Ritzy City with her gloopy hand, 'is Brollywood, where they make all the TV shows and films and things. It's where all the famous witches live.'

'AND ME,' said Fran. 'I'm famous. I live there. And I work there too, on my excellent TV shows, including *Witch Wars*.

'Witch Wars is a TV show?' Tiga asked.

Fran raised a hand in the air. 'I'll explain all that when we get back upstairs where we are meant to be, rather than down here where we are not.'

'Not what?' Peggy asked.

'Meant to be,' Fran said.

'Meant to be what?' Peggy asked.

Fran scrunched up her little face. 'Meant to be here!'

'We're meant to be here?' Peggy asked with a smile.

'PEGGY!' Fran shouted.

Tiga noticed there seemed to be a lot more pipes painted in the sky in Brollywood than there were in Ritzy City.

Fran followed her gaze. 'Everyone carries umbrellas in Brollywood,' she said. 'It's quite wet there what with all the pipes, and – oh! – I smell something, the stench of more competitors …'

Tiga couldn't smell anything. She looked at Peggy, whose nose was scrunched up and sniffing too, but she just shrugged.

'Come on!' Fran said, making a beeline for the sofa. Tiga glanced back at the map. She hadn't had nearly enough time to see all of Sinkville, and there was a lot of Sinkville to see.

'You can come back any time,' Fran said with a smile, 'apart from on Wednesdays. This room doesn't exist on Wednesdays.'

# The Witch
# Wars Witches

Back in the entrance hall, Tiga watched as Fran hovered in front of a crowd of witches. Her tiny eyes were fixed on a very tall and solid witch with long hair that hung from her hat all the way down to her knees.

'Lizzie Beast,' said Fran in an uncharacteristically evil tone. 'How is your *mother* doing?'

Lizzie Beast nodded. 'Good, thanks, Fran. Filming today.'

'Lizzie Beast's mum is a camera operator in Brollywood,' whispered Peggy. 'She and Lizzie are both famously clumsy –'

Tiga watched as Lizzie Beast swung her arm and accidentally smacked one of the other witches in the face.

'Once when Lizzie Beast's mum was filming a TV programme with a bunch of fairies about why glittery dust is very important, she sat on one of the fairies and squashed her. It kick-started the Fairy Riots.'

'Oh no,' said Tiga. 'What happened?'

'Almost nothing,' said Peggy, shaking her head. 'They flew around chanting, "WHAT DO WE WANT? NOT TO BE SQUASHED! AND WE'D ALSO QUITE LIKE A PONY!" Only one of the fairies was yelling the pony bit, which annoyed all the others and the riots soon turned into a tiny flying ball of fairies all pulling each other's hair and shouting, "Stop saying the pony bit, Alison!" You'll meet most of the fairies later. They help with Witch Wars. There are hardly any left in Sinkville these days.'

'Oh no,' said Tiga. 'What happened?'

'Almost nothing,' said Peggy, shaking her head. 'When a spell was invented to make fairies big, most of them decided to do that, rather than be small and squashable. It's probably for the best. I don't know if you've noticed, but fairies can be pretty annoying.'

There was a tiny cough.

'Apart from *you*, Fran,' Peggy quickly added.

'You might find fairies annoying,' Fran said, wagging her finger, 'but without us you wouldn't have …'

'… screechy voices?' Peggy guessed.

'Dust!' Fran screeched, shooting a big dollop of the stuff at Lizzie Beast's face.

All the witches in the room blinked at Fran, and Tiga stared at all the witches. She had positioned herself half-way behind a stone statue of a jolly young witch sitting in a bin.

On any other day she would've asked why on earth they had made a witch-in-a-bin statue, but on this day she didn't want to ask anything. She felt a lot like she had on her first day at school, only surrounded by witches and an odd ranting fairy.

Fran took a tiny pen out of her pocket and scribbled *Lizzie Beast* in the air, with a tick. The letters exploded, sending a silly amount of glittery dust shooting through the air like fireworks. After the dust had cleared, the

letters, which now looked burnt and spindly, dropped to the ground.

'Is that really necessary?' a little witch squeaked.

Fran raised her finger in the air, ready to shoot more glittery dust.

'OK, OK,' the little witch said, her hands in the air as she backed off.

'Patty Pigeon,' said Fran, glaring at her.

The tiny witch with plaited pigtails sticking out the sides of her hat nodded. 'I'm Patty from the Towers.'

Fran smiled and wrote *Patty Pigeon* in the air with her pen. All the witches ducked as glittery dust burst from the letters.

'NEXT!' Fran shouted.

There was no missing the next one. She was leaning against the wall dressed in the puffiest skirt Tiga had ever seen. It looked more like a trifle than a piece of clothing.

'I have zero interest in being here,' the witch said loudly, scanning the room for a reaction. Fran was bobbing up and down excitedly in front of her.

39

'Oh, Fluffanora! It's so great to see you here, and dressed in *such* style! How is Mrs Brew? Does she mention me all the time?'

'Um … no, I don't think so,' Fluffanora said. She glanced over at Tiga. 'Nice jeans.'

Tiga wasn't sure whether she was being kind or mean.

Fran was whizzing about, back and forth, trying to catch Fluffanora's eye. 'We have met before, at your mother's shop. I'm … well, I'm quite famous.'

Peggy moved closer to Tiga, who had been slowly

moving further and further behind the statue. 'That's Fluffanora Brew, the daughter of Mrs Brew, the fashion designer. There are always pictures of her in *Toad* magazine. They say she's the best-dressed girl in Ritzy City.'

'Fluffanora, your mother didn't mention the diamond-encrusted skirt that she designed especially for me when I won the award for Best and Only Fairy Film of the Year, did she?' asked Fran with a huge grin plastered on her face.

Fluffanora shook her head.

Fran's grin shrank a bit. 'Or the little shoes with the velvet bows and the parrot face ... designed just for me ... no?'

Fluffanora craned her neck past Fran and pointed at Tiga behind the statue. 'You know, we don't have jeans in Ritzy City – you can only get them above the pipes. It's cool to see them in real life.'

Tiga felt all shy and did a sort of half wave from behind the statue. Then, for good measure, she stuck one leg out as if to display the jeans to the rest of the room.

Two girls pushed past Fluffanora.

'Ah, yes, the twins,' said Fran. 'Welcome, Milly and Molly.'

Tiga caught the eye of one of them and smiled, but the girl just bared her teeth as the other cackled.

'Right,' said Fran, twirling in the air. 'All nine of you are here so we can begin! Oh, it's been nine long years since I've done this!'

'Um, Fran,' said Tiga, taking a brave, deep breath and stepping out from behind the statue.

'What is it, Tiga?'

Tiga looked around the room at all the witches staring back at her. 'Um, it's just you said *nine* witches, but there are only seven of us.'

Fran glanced at her tiny watch. 'LATE!' she roared, just as the chandelier in the hall began to shake. At first it seemed to Tiga that Fran's shouting had made it happen, but it was something far worse than the shrill squeak of a fairy. The lights dimmed, the witch statue slid further down into the bin and the pictures on the walls began to sway.

The door burst open.

It banged loudly off the wall, making everyone jump. Then it slammed shut again, which made everyone laugh.

But they stopped laughing when it creaked open and they saw who was standing behind it.

Well, not standing exactly. One was sitting on the back of another witch, and the other was levitating in the air.

# 7

## The Rules

'Oh my FROGS, are those *jeans*?' said Aggie Hoof as she dismounted the witch and dropped her *Toad* magazine on the floor. 'Well, we all know who's from above the pipes!'

She cackled. Milly and Molly joined in. But Felicity Bat had been distracted by something else. That something else was Peggy.

'Well, if it isn't Piggy Pigwiggle,' she said. 'I'm surprised you even showed up.'

'Ha! Piggy's here! Piggy's here!' Aggie Hoof chanted.

Peggy's face crumpled. 'It's *Peggy*, actually.'

'No, it's not. It's Piggy,' said Felicity Bat.

'Do you know these girls?' Tiga asked.

Peggy sighed. 'I go to school with them up on Pearl

Peak. It's the best school in Sinkville and my gran saved for years to send me there. It costs a lot of sinkels. I come from the Docks, which is nothing like Pearl Peak.'

'The Docks are for losers,' said Aggie Hoof, butting in. 'And Pearl Peak is not. It's the oldest and most important part of Sinkville. The first witch to land below the pipes landed in Pearl Peak. The witch-shaped hole she made when she landed is still there. And we have Sinkville's only roller coaster, and a castle and also some sky and stuff.'

'Almost every winner of Witch Wars has come from Pearl Peak,' said Felicity Bat proudly. 'And that's the way it will stay.'

'I just find Pearl Peak so insanely boring,' said Fluffanora from the chair in which she was now slumped. 'Yes, there's a castle, but it's so cold and snowy and dark up there, and there are too many mean witches. Also the clothes are weird.'

Aggie Hoof gasped. 'YOU THINK THE *CLOTHES* ARE WEIRD? Who in all of Sinkville do you think you are?'

'I'm Fluffanora Brew.'

Aggie Hoof paused and then smiled in that sickly-sweet way only terrible people can smile. 'Oh frogtrumpets! I didn't recognise you in the flesh. You are fashion royalty … according to *Toad*, which means you definitely are. I *love* your outfit, it's just wonderful to meet you!' She skipped over and gave Fluffanora a huge hug. 'Let's be friends.'

Fluffanora shook her head. 'I'm afraid I pick my friends like I pick my hats. *Very* carefully. I never choose hideous ones.'

Aggie Hoof scoffed and spluttered and spun on her heel to face Tiga. 'What are you smiling at, Weirdo from Above the Pipes?'

Tiga stopped smiling.

'Who's that lady she was sitting on?' Tiga asked Peggy.

'I love idiot witches from above the pipes,' Felicity Bat said with a smirk.

Aggie Hoof cackled.

'Witches usually travel by cleaning equipment,' Peggy hurriedly explained. 'You know, brooms, hoovers,

small feather dusters under each foot …'

'And cleaners,' said Aggie Hoof. 'Karen is my cleaner, so I travel on her, *obviously*.'

'She's the only one who does that …' Peggy said.

Fran finished scribbling Felicity Bat's and Aggie Hoof's names in the air and chuckled as glittery dust exploded everywhere.

Felicity Bat rolled her eyes and muttered, 'She's such a glittery ball of boring happiness.'

'Ladies,' Fran said with a smile, 'it's getting late – we must get to the rules. This way!'

Tiga watched as Aggie Hoof pushed herself to the front and tottered after Fran, closely followed by Felicity Bat and the others. Peggy nudged Tiga forward. 'Come on, Tiga. You don't want to be left behind.'

Down the corridor they went, past statues and door after door, until they reached a really small one. Behind that lay another long corridor lined with more statues and doors. They went through an even smaller door that led to a room lined with thousands and thousands of grey books. Shimmering black ladders stretched

from floor to ceiling.

Fran soared through the air to the 'W' section and pushed a book.

'And now,' she said, 'I give you, THE RULES!'

The bookcases began to shake and, with a bang, all the grey books changed colour. Deep turquoise, bright orange, delicious purple – all with beautiful patterned spines.

'This is the only colour that remains in all of Sinkville,' said Fran with a sigh.

The eight witches stood with their mouths hanging open.

'I've never seen colours like this before,' said Peggy, taking a step towards the books. 'I've heard about them, but I've never seen them.'

'We have all the colours above the pipes,' said Tiga, who was a bit confused.

'Oh, *we have all the colours above the pipes*,' Felicity Bat said mockingly.

'During what has become known as the Big Exit,' Fran explained, 'some very bad witches left Sinkville

48

forever for a new life in the world above the pipes and they took all the colour with them. But they couldn't touch the colour in this room. These books contain all of Sinkville's history. And they couldn't take that.'

'But why did they leave?' Tiga asked.

'No one really knows. Most witches believe it was because they wanted to terrorise the children up there. There was a trend for sneaking up the pipes and scaring them silly. Celia Crayfish went up and invented home-work and Brussels sprouts, which have tortured children ever since.

'Anyway, when they left, they took everything with them. It wasn't just the colour. They took their houses and shops too. That's why there are buildings missing all over Sinkville.'

Tiga ran her hands across the coloured spines.

'Each book you see here is the story of a witch who ruled Sinkville,' Fran went on, slapping Tiga's hand. 'Every nine years, nine witches, all nine years of age, are chosen to compete in Witch Wars. The winner, one of you, will be the next Top Witch, the witch who will rule

49

over all of Sinkville. In these books you'll find stories about all kinds of witches: some good, some bad, some boring, but all important. The last Top Witch, Big Sue, was very nice and did many great things, like planting more trees and giving money to charity and letting bins speak again. And then there are the evil Top Witches, like Celia Crayfish.' Fran rolled her eyes. 'She invented Annual Present-Burning Day, the day after Christmas.'

'Celia Crayfish was magnificent,' said Felicity Bat. 'And she was my grandmother.'

'Oh yes,' said Fran. 'I'd forgotten about that. She was very good – at being dreadful.'

That seemed to please Felicity Bat.

'Every Top Witch who has ruled this place stood in this very room on the eve of their Witch Wars, knowing that, if they won, their story would end up in one of these books.'

Fran did a series of somersaults and bowed.

Everyone reluctantly clapped.

'Now,' she said, 'as most of you know, the Top Witch will live here in Linden House. For years this place was

a mound of mud, then a witch built a small straw hut on it. That blew away pretty quickly and someone said, "Let's just build a massive house." And so they did. And here we are, in the grandest residence in all of Ritzy City. Home to Sinkville's most important artworks, its biggest staircase, its weirdest statues, and Pat the chef, who no one has seen in fifty years, but she must still be alive down there because food keeps popping up from the kitchen.'

'Why choose a nine-year-old?' asked Tiga. 'Above the pipes they would never allow a nine-year-old to make the rules.'

Fran soared through the air and landed on Tiga's shoulder. 'Nine-year-olds, my dear, see the world in a brilliant and wonderful way. And they are quite small. The smaller the person, the better they almost certainly are.'

'You're just saying that because you're *really* small,' said Aggie Hoof.

Fran shot like a torpedo through the air and pinched Aggie's nose.

'So what exactly happens in Witch Wars?' Tiga asked.

Felicity Bat cackled. 'Why do you want to know what happens, Tiga? So you can *win*?'

Tiga looked sheepishly at her holey trainers.

'I'm getting to that,' said Fran. 'Tomorrow, each of you will be presented with a shrivelled head.'

'Yuck,' said Patty Pigeon.

'Wimp,' sneered Molly.

'That head keeps you in the game,' said Fran. 'If your shrivelled head is crushed, you are OUT. You can try to crush the shrivelled heads of your opponents if you want to knock them out, but to win you must solve four Witch Wars riddles, in order, and make it to the end of the game. Skip a riddle and the end will never appear.'

'So it's not actually a war?' Tiga asked.

Fran shook her head. 'Witches used to fight to the death, but eventually someone realised that was nuts and now we just play a highly competitive game instead. But we kept the name because it's catchy.'

All the witches were listening intently, and nodding –

apart from Felicity Bat, who had levitated up to the top shelf and was reading *The Celia Crayfish Years*.

'Each of you will be assigned a fairy, and each fairy will carry a camera, which the team in Brollywood will use to broadcast Witch Wars to all of Sinkville. You will be watched throughout the land, so expect that everywhere you go people will know who you are. You must use your magic and your wits to make your way to the end before the other witches. There are no more rules. Some witches have won by playing fairly and others have won by cheating.'

'Grandmother did that,' said Felicity Bat, waving the Celia Crayfish book in the air.

'Yes, well, she was a big, stup– oh, look at the time! We must have dinner,' Fran chirped. 'Back we go.'

Felicity Bat soared through the air and shoved Peggy out of the way.

'Watch where you're going!' Tiga shouted. She instantly realised her mistake.

'Did you just yell at my Fel-Fel?' Aggie Hoof said, stepping closer to Tiga.

'I'll handle it,' said Felicity Bat, moving so close to Tiga that they were almost nose to pointy-warty nose. 'You are nothing. You are a nobody from above the pipes. I'm going to knock you out of the competition first. And your little Piggy too.'

'And you look stupid in those jeans,' said Aggie Hoof. 'Everyone is going to laugh at you. And Piggy, how *old* is your hat?'

'It … it belonged to my great-great-great-gran,' said Peggy, taking the dusty old hat off her head.

'That's disgusting,' said Aggie Hoof.

'You know,' said Fluffanora, stepping into the middle. 'You're right, Aggie Goof, or whatever your name is.'

'HOOF!' Aggie Hoof yelled.

'Right, Hoof,' said Fluffanora dismissively. 'The jeans are no good for Witch Wars. Tiga, why don't we go to my mum's shop and get you a dress.'

Tiga's eyes lit up. 'Really?'

'And a new hat for Peggy,' said Fluffanora.

'THAT'S THE BEST IDEA I'VE HEARD IN ALL MY LIFE,' roared Fran. 'Can I come too?'

'But then who will look after all the other witches?' asked Fluffanora.

Fran stared at the group. 'Frogsknees. I'll have to stay.'

And so off the three of them went, arm in arm to Brew's, as Felicity Bat and Aggie Hoof huddled together and whispered like evil witches making a terrible, terrible plan.

# Inside Brew's

Linden House grew darker and the huge chandeliers that hung low from the ceilings flickered into life as Tiga stepped out on to the bustling street. The air was warm and all along the road little lanterns floated about next to the towering buildings. Glamorous, chattering witches glided past and the little cafés that lined the streets were full to the brim with witches eating and laughing and a witch who had just fallen off her chair.

The one thing Tiga had really wanted to do since hearing about it was to see inside Brew's. She clutched Peggy's arm and grinned.

'Don't get excited,' Fluffanora said. 'It's nothing special.' She climbed the white marble steps and slotted a little black key into the lock.

When the door swung open, Tiga's mouth swung open too. Brew's was huge. It was sparkly. It looked like an elephant-sized Fran had exploded in there.

It was FABULOUS!

Fluffanora glided on ahead, past hundreds of little witches dressed in black dresses. 'They're stocking the shelves for tomorrow,' she called back. 'Only I'm allowed in here this late at night.'

To the left was a huge wall of shelves lined with beautiful shoes and over in the opposite corner was a group of witches laying out silky gloves. An old witch with a beehive of white hair was climbing a ladder on the far wall, throwing scarves down to a group of young witches wearing puffy little skirts. A tall, spindly witch sailed past Tiga on a cart filled with wide-brimmed hats. She waved as she passed.

Fluffanora ran along the rails of clothes, throwing dresses into the arms of one of the assistants.

'Don't forget to put the new umbrellas out!' someone cried from behind Tiga. 'We have some special customers from Brollywood visiting tomorrow.'

'Will someone unpack the crystal handbags?' shouted another.

Tiga turned to find Fluffanora standing right behind her, holding a beautiful black lace dress. Next to her stood an assistant. Well, Tiga *thought* it was an assistant, because she could see some little legs sticking out from under the huge pile of fancy fabric.

'Yes. I think this is the one. Come on,' Fluffanora said, holding up the dress.

'So … you … don't want any of these … no?' came a voice from under the pile. The little legs wobbled.

'Nah,' Fluffanora said, leading Tiga towards the changing rooms. Tiga looked back and saw the little legs buckle and all the dresses land in a heap on the floor.

'Peggy, go and pick a hat,' said Fluffanora, taking the black lace frock off the hanger. Peggy nearly choked.

'A hat? I thought you were just *saying* that so Fran would let me go with you.'

'I never just say anything. Go and pick one. Take any one you like.'

Peggy started making a weird noise; it went something like, 'Ohfrogeeeeeeeeeeeee!' and then she bounded off towards the hat department.

Tiga was thinking how nice Fluffanora was as the witch zipped up the dress and yanked it and pulled it.

'Perfect,' she said, spinning Tiga round to face the mirror.

Tiga almost didn't recognise herself. She smoothed the layers of lace on the skirt.

'And now all you need is –' Fluffanora began.

'A HAT!' Peggy cried, sliding over to Tiga and slapping a huge wide-brimmed hat on her head. Peggy was still wearing her old hat.

'You didn't find a hat?' Fluffanora asked.

Peggy shook her head. 'They're all lovely. The best hats I've ever seen! This one I'm wearing, I think, has bugs living in it, but my gran gave it to me, and it feels a bit special, so I might just stick with this one.'

Fluffanora smiled at her.

'What are you doing?' came a voice behind them.

Tiga spun round. The voice belonged to an older witch wearing a long polka-dot dress. She'd teamed it with a slouchy black cardigan and a massive pair of earrings. Her hair was twisted into a loose bun and secured with a paintbrush.

'Oh, hi, Mum. Just getting some clothes for my Witch Wars friends,' Fluffanora said.

Tiga pulled the hat off her head and hid it behind her back.

'Of course, dear,' Fluffanora's mum said, smiling at Tiga. 'You'll need shoes too'. She picked some black ones with little pearls and big white and grey stripes on the heels and passed them to Tiga.

'Thank you,' Tiga gushed.

'You're Tiga, from above the pipes, aren't you? I'm Mrs Brew.'

Tiga smiled, and almost bowed, but decided against it.

'Well, this must be quite a shock!' Mrs Brew said. 'I hear it's very different up there. I hope you're enjoying it in Ritzy City?'

'She *is*, Mum,' Fluffanora huffed. 'You can take a crystal handbag too, if you want, Tiga? I designed those.'

'Ah,' Peggy said, looking worried. 'About them. You see, in my excitement to get to the hats, I'm so sorry but I might have broken a few of those … and by a few I mean somewhere in the region of twenty.' She pulled a sort of 'oops' face.

Mrs Brew, much to Tiga's relief, laughed.

'Why don't you all go to Clutterbucks?' Mrs Brew suggested.

'What's Clutterbucks?' Tiga and Peggy said at the same time.

Fluffanora and Mrs Brew smiled at each other.

'Clutterbucks it is,' said Fluffanora. 'But first, Tiga … could I try on your jeans?'

# Clutterbucks

'Maybe we should go back to Linden House,' said Peggy. 'It's getting late.'

'NEVER!' cried Fluffanora, skipping down the street in her jeans.

Tiga laughed and raced after her. 'Come on, Peggy!' she called back.

As Peggy came lolloping along behind, Tiga realised something. Ritzy City was the best place on Earth. (If it was somewhere on Earth.) And she wanted to stay.

All the Witch Wars stuff, the fighting, the cackling, the Felicity Bats, had made Tiga worry that Ritzy City was not the place for her. But she loved this.

Fluffanora weaved in and out of the crowds of witches, who were all very amused by her jeans. And Tiga skipped along next to her in her dress and massive hat and for the first time felt like a proper Ritzy City witch.

They took a sharp left down an alleyway that at first seemed like a dead end. But hidden in the shadows was a tiny door and an even tinier window. Fluffanora knocked seven times then drummed her fingers once, and then knocked one final time.

A plump, rosy-cheeked witch in a huge wide-brimmed hat flung the door open.

'Fluffanora! You're here! SOMETHING HAS HAPPENED TO YOUR LEGS!' she cried.

'Jeans, Mrs Clutterbuck. It's the fashion above the pipes.'

Mrs Clutterbuck raised an eyebrow. '*Beans?*'

'JEANS,' said Fluffanora. 'Anyway, we're all doing that stupid Witch Wars thing tomorrow and could really do with a Clutterbucks. These are my friends, Peggy and Tiga.'

'Witch Wars, you say? Well, come in! Come in, dears!'

Behind the little door Tiga expected to see a tiny cave of a place – maybe some wooden tables and chairs, but instead a huge white light spelling out CLUTTERBUCKS swung from the ceiling, and all up the old wonky walls were ornate tables and chairs that looked as if they were floating.

Witches cackled and laughed and drank out of elaborate glasses, and steam billowed and puffed from little machines dotted about the place.

'Clutterbucks is a secret café – only important fashion people are allowed inside. They make the best bubbly drinks in town and some very excellent cakes,' Fluffanora explained. 'These two have never been here before,' she said to the witch who was showing them to their seats.

Tiga looked back at Peggy and laughed. Her eyes were huge, her mouth was open, her hands were smacked against her cheeks.

Over in the corner, Tiga saw a group of witches

having fun waving their hands and changing the colour of another witch's skirt, from black, to white, to grey …

'Oooh, grey is nice,' they said.

… To spotty, to stripy, to INVISIBLE.

The witch covered her frilly pants with her hands. 'Stop that!' she yelled.

The witch waitress led them up some winding stairs and pointed at one of the tables floating nearby. 'We float 'em so we have more space,' she said, handing them each a menu.

Tiga pulled a chair over and sat down shakily. It wobbled and tipped from left to right. She grabbed her hat with one hand and steadied the chair with the other.

Peggy leapt on to her chair with such force that it spun madly in a circle, sending her hat flying across the room and straight into someone's cake.

'So sorry,' Peggy mouthed across the room.

Fluffanora just sat down.

# CLUTTERBUCKS

Makers of the best bubbly drinks since
winks were invented

Ritzy Original – 5 sinkels
The Witching Whirl – 8 sinkels
Flat-Hat Fizz – 6 sinkels
The We-Hate-Celia-Crayfish Cocktail – 6 sinkels
Witch Wars Mix – 5 sinkels
The Big Exit Bubble Mix – 5 sinkels
Brilliant Big Sue Supreme – 8 sinkels
BOOM* – 9,000 sinkels

*WARNING: This drink transports you back in time
for ten minutes to Ritzy City a hundred years ago.
(Two hundred years ago if you drink it through
your nose.)

Mrs Clutterbuck appeared at their table carrying a tray
of glasses filled with a shimmering black liquid, each
with a huge striped straw.

'Here you go, dears! Enjoy your Clutterbucks! I thought you'd like the Witch Wars one,' she said with a wink. 'Your snack,' she added, nodding at a massive three-tier cake that was wobbling through the air, 'is on its way.'

Peggy took a huge swig of her drink and made a massive slurping noise.

'I love this place!' said Tiga.

'Yeah? It's all right, I suppose,' said Fluffanora.

'You're so cool!' gushed Peggy. '*And* you have such a unique name.'

Tiga nodded, but Fluffanora shook her head and took a sip of her drink.

'It's not my real name. When I was four, I demanded they change it. I used to be called Anna, but Fluffanora seemed cooler at the time. Sometimes I wish they hadn't given me *everything* I wanted.'

Peggy cackled and nearly fell off her chair. 'Oh frog-pies, that's hilarious! You changed your name! TO FLUFFANORA!'

Fluffanora paused and looked sternly at Peggy for a

worrying second, but then cackled too. It was the first time Tiga had ever seen her laugh.

The witches at the table next to them burst into a chorus of cackles too. They were, much to Tiga's surprise, cackling at their spoons.

'What are they doing?' she asked.

'Watching TV,' said Peggy.

'On *spoons*?' Tiga spluttered.

'Of course. Why, where do you watch TV, Tiga?'

'Well, on a TV,' Tiga said.

'Yes, but where do you make the TV appear?'

Tiga had no idea what Peggy was talking about.

'So you can't do the TV spell?' Fluffanora asked as she waved at Mrs Clutterbuck and ordered another drink.

Tiga didn't really want to admit that she didn't know any spells.

'She doesn't know any spells,' said Peggy, patting Tiga on the back, 'but I'm going to teach her some.'

'Witch Wars is going to be tricky if you don't know any spells!' said Fluffanora. She must've seen Tiga's face

crumple, because she quickly added, 'Not that you really *need* spells for Witch Wars …'

'You don't?' Tiga asked.

It sort of sounded to her like you really did.

'Why don't you teach her the TV spell, Peggy?' said Fluffanora.

'YES!' Peggy cried, attempting to stand up but then remembering she was on a floating chair. 'Where would you like to watch TV?'

Tiga glanced around Clutterbucks. Only a couple of tables in front of them sat a witch scratching her bald head.

'On her head!' Tiga joked.

'Oh, OK,' Peggy said casually, 'look at her head and repeat after me: TV.'

'We can make a TV on the back of her head?' Tiga asked. 'I was *joking*.'

'Of course we can,' said Peggy. 'Now, repeat: TV.'

'TV,' said Tiga.

'TV,' Peggy said again.

'TV,' said Tiga.

'TV, TV, TV.'

'What? This is –' Tiga started.

'Oh, just say it,' said Fluffanora.

'TV, TV, TV,' Tiga mumbled. And then, just like that, a moving image appeared on the back of the bald woman's head!

'Oh, you don't want that channel!' Peggy giggled. 'That's Fairy Five – it's all just stuff for fairies.'

The presenter fairy was pointing at a large window and shaking her finger, as some fairies smacked into it. *WATCH OUT FOR WINDOWS* scrolled along the bottom of the screen.

'To change the channel, you click your fingers,' said Peggy. But, before Tiga could, the bald witch pulled a hat on to her head and the screen disappeared.

'That's why people tend to watch it on spoons, because it's easier,' Peggy said. 'Witch Wars will be the biggest thing on TV.'

'Psst,' said one of the witches at a nearby table. She nudged her friend and pointed at Tiga. 'Witch Wars witches.'

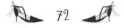

Tiga smiled at them, which made them giggle.

'Oh, let's not do Witch Wars,' Fluffanora cried. 'It's so stupid.'

'But if you win you get to live in Linden House!' said Peggy.

'Linden House is about five times smaller than my house,' said Fluffanora. 'And I mean the playhouse in my garden that I've had since I was two.'

'It's huge to me!' said Peggy, sipping her Clutterbucks. 'And if you win you get to make the rules and make things nice for people.'

Tiga watched as Peggy pulled a tattered little notebook out of her pocket.

'I've been thinking about the rules for as long as I can remember. Every time I think of a good one, I write it down. And if I ever meet someone who is sad I write their name in here just in case I ever do become Top Witch, and then I won't forget to help them.'

Tiga smiled as Peggy stuffed the notebook back in her pocket.

'Ugh, that's so boring, though!' said Fluffanora,

throwing her hands in the air. 'Who cares about other people? Let's just hide out in Clutterbucks and let one of the other witches win.'

Tiga loved Clutterbucks, and the thought of making a fool of herself on the back of a spoon wasn't really her idea of fun. And, now that she thought about it, she was never going to learn enough magic by the morning to actually win.

'Yeah!' Tiga cried. 'Let's hang out in Clutterbucks FOREVER!'

She clinked her glass against Fluffanora's.

Fluffanora winked. 'That's the spirit!'

Peggy scrunched up her face into a horrified little ball. 'But, Tiga, don't you want to compete? Don't you owe it to the person who put you forward for Witch Wars?'

Tiga put her drink down on the table. 'Wait, someone put my name down for this?'

Peggy nodded. 'Of course! You have to be nominated by another Sinkville witch. The names of the first nine nine-year-old witches nominated in Sinkville on the day the Top Witch's reign ends are chosen to compete.'

'Who nominated you?' Fluffanora asked Peggy.

'My gran. She thinks I'm brilliant at everything, but I think that's got a lot to do with the fact that she loves me and is almost completely blind. Who nominated you?'

Fluffanora shook her head. 'My mum. She thinks it's a good way for me to make some friends. I had to remind her it's a competition based on an ancient war.'

They both looked at Tiga, who was staring blankly back at them.

'Who nominated you, Tiga?' Peggy asked.

Tiga shook her head. 'It's impossible. I don't know any witches. I'd never met a witch until I came here today.'

'Someone knows you,' said Fluffanora, finishing off her drink.

'Who?' Tiga asked.

But Peggy and Fluffanora had no idea.

# Feathers

On the way back to Linden House the wind whipped around them and Tiga tried desperately to study the face of every witch she passed on the street, hoping she'd see someone familiar. Cackles rang out around her and huge wide-brimmed hats shot past.

'Are you OK?' Peggy asked as they reached Linden House.

There was a squeal as Fran shot out of the letterbox. 'LET ME SEE! LET ME SEE!'

She screeched to a halt in front of Tiga.

'FABULOUS,' she concluded, before adding, 'You're just in time to pick beds.'

Inside, it was difficult to see anything through all the grey feathers that were floating down in big clumps from upstairs.

'I WANT THAT BED!'

'I SAID THIS ROOM WAS MINE!'

'STOP EATING MY PILLOW!'

'There's been some debate about who should sleep where,' said Fran, as an especially large feather soared down and knocked her to the ground.

Upstairs, Felicity Bat was levitating along the corridor as Aggie Hoof trotted along behind her.

'Fel-Fel, can we sleep in the same room?'

'No.'

'What if I promise not to read *Toad* out loud, Fel-Fel?'

'No.'

Tiga tugged Peggy's arm. 'How does Felicity Bat do that? Is it like the TV spell?'

Peggy rolled her eyes. 'Levitating? No, not at all. It's an almost-impossible spell – barely any witches can do it. They say she's gifted.'

To the right, Molly was in a room hitting Lizzie Beast on the head with a pillow and Milly was swinging Patty Pigeon around by her pigtails.

'GIRLS!' Fran snapped. 'The rooms are almost exactly the same. Well, apart from the *huge* one upstairs …'

Everyone stopped and stared at Fran. Then, as if someone had hit the play button, they all shot up the stairs, pushing and shoving each other.

Tiga, Peggy and Fluffanora watched them go.

'There isn't even a bed up there,' Fran said with a chuckle. 'There might be an angry cat, though …'

Fluffanora wandered into a room and pressed a hand on the bed to check it was soft enough. 'Night, ladies,' she said, just as the sound of a furious cat screeching came from upstairs.

Fran smiled. 'Angry cat,' she said. 'So very, very angry.'

Peggy and Tiga wandered along the corridor, slipping on feathers as they went. They decided on two light-grey rooms that sat side by side and were connected by a large door.

They said goodnight and for the first time since Fran had marched into the crumbly old shed, Tiga was alone.

On her bed was a little box and in it was a black nightie, a black toothbrush, a black tube of toothpaste and some foot cream, labelled *Flappy Flora's Floral Foot Cream*.

Tiga curled up in bed surrounded by the hundreds of portraits of witches that hung on the walls. She wondered if she knew any of them, or if maybe this was all a big mistake and she wasn't really a witch. Maybe she was the wrong Tiga Whicabim. Her eyes darted from one witch to another, and settled on a terrifying one. A lace veil covered her face and you could just make out the fangs through it.

It was just at that moment that Peggy came bursting through the door.

'I JUST REALISED YOU MIGHT NEED SOME EXTRA FOOT CREAM. HERE, HAVE MINE!' she yelled, making Tiga jump.

'Um, I think I'm OK for foot cream, Pegs …'

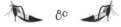

'Oh, OK, it's not actually about the foot cream … Can I sleep in here? There's a load of creepy paintings in my room.' She looked to where Tiga was looking. 'Argh! Your paintings are SO MUCH WORSE! I didn't even think that was possible, but look! It is!'

Tiga burst out laughing.

It was almost a cackle.

She patted the bed and Peggy jumped on to it and handed Tiga her tub of foot cream. 'They don't make that stuff any more because they realised "Flappy Flora's Floral Foot Cream" is really difficult to say.'

Tiga smiled and sniffed the cream. It smelled like flowers and feet. 'Sinkville is full of such funny things,' she said.

'What's it like above the pipes?' asked Peggy as she wriggled under the covers.

Tiga thought about it for a moment and said, 'Different, but not better. I live with a terrible old woman called Miss Heks. She found me in the sink in her shed when I was a baby. No one knew who I belonged to or where I had come from, so she took

me in. But she hates children, and me most of all. I practically live in the shed – it's the only place I can go to get away from her.'

'That's terrible,' said Peggy. 'She sounds worse than a bad witch!'

'Well,' said Tiga, pointing at the scary witch painting. 'I'm not sure she's worse than *that*. But I love it here much more than up there above the pipes. I want to stay forever.'

Peggy smiled a sympathetic smile and patted Tiga's arm. 'You'll never have to go back. We'll make sure of it. I'll help you learn spells and we can work together to win Witch Wars!'

Tiga grinned. Witch Wars wasn't so scary with Peggy around.

'How many spells do you know?'

'Almost eight,' said Peggy proudly. 'And four of them sometimes work!'

Tiga groaned and slid further under the covers.

'KAREN!' they heard Aggie Hoof scream. 'You sleep downstairs.'

'It'll be cold down there,' whispered Tiga. 'Maybe we could see if Karen wants to sleep in here with us?'

Peggy nodded. 'Excellent idea!' She took out her notebook and Tiga watched as, on the page titled *People Peggy Must Remember to Help*, she scribbled *Karen*.

A bit of hair gunk fell from Peggy's head and splattered on the page, smudging it almost completely.

# Tiga Changes
# Her Mind

NEEEEEEOOOOOOWWWAAAAHHHHSSSH was the noise Tiga woke up to the following morning.

'Come on, come on, we don't have all day – well, I suppose we do have all day, unless we die, but let's not think about death or take a really long time to get ready, OK?' Fran said, zooming around the bedroom.

It was a lot for Tiga to deal with at seven o'clock in the morning.

'Downstairs for breakfast, please,' said Fran before shooting out of the door.

Tiga did up the zip on her Brew's dress and adjusted her hat.

'*KAAAARRREEEEN?*' Aggie Hoof roared from the hallway.

84

'I hope one of you two wins,' Karen whispered, before scuttling off.

Peggy bounded after her. 'Come on, Tiga! BREAK-FAST!'

Tiga was about to run after them when she noticed a witch's face appear in the window. As they were on the third floor, Tiga was pretty surprised to see a face hovering there, and so she squealed. The witch waved, took a photo and suddenly disappeared.

When Tiga peered down, she saw the witch lying in

a heap on the pavement on top of a broken ladder, surrounded by about a million witches in huge wide-brimmed hats. All at once they looked up.

'IT'S THE TIGA WITCH!' someone screeched.

'THE ONE FROM ABOVE THE PIPES!' another cried.

Tiga nervously backed away and ran down the corridor. She took the stairs two at a time and landed with a thud in the hallway. She followed the clink of forks and the chatter of witches beyond the entrance hall to a large dining room. Fluffanora was already there, picking at a muffin. Peggy was next to her, spilling cereal everywhere.

Fran was zooming around barking orders.

'Where is Tiga?'

Tiga hid behind the door.

'Mupmairs,' Peggy said.

'Is that some sort of shop I don't know about?' Fran asked.

'Upstairs,' Fluffanora said.

'Well, I shall go and get her!'

86

Fran zoomed past, tutting.

It was then that Tiga made her decision. She didn't want to compete in Witch Wars. And so she dived into the empty little sitting room with the flowery sofa.

Fran flew into the room, but before she could speak Tiga raised a hand and said as firmly as she could, 'Fran, I am not going to compete in Witch Wars. I am going to watch it in Clutterbucks on the back of a spoon.'

Fran slumped over in the air and sighed. 'I'm afraid you can't do that, dear.' She smoothed out the ruffles on her skirt and took a seat in the air. 'Either you compete or I have to take you home.'

Tiga held on to the sofa to steady herself. It hadn't occurred to her that she'd have to go back to Miss Heks. 'I can't stay?'

Fran shook her head. 'We have to return you after Witch Wars. Well, unless …'

'Unless what?' Tiga asked eagerly.

'Unless you win and become Top Witch.'

Tiga took a step back and plonked herself down on the sofa. Her legs felt heavy, her heart felt rubbish, her

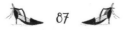

head felt like it was doing a somersault. She'd completely forgotten the sofa was no ordinary sofa!

It flipped round and she found herself sitting in front of the map.

She stared at it.

'It would be nice if you could stay,' Fran said as she appeared behind Tiga.

Tiga didn't take her eyes off the map. 'Fran?' she asked. 'Who nominated me for Witch Wars?'

Fran shrugged. 'Oh, they don't tell me that. *Not* because I'm not important. No, I'm *very* important. I am the face of the show. But they don't tell me the finer details.'

'Who are *they*?' Tiga asked.

'The producers in Brollywood,' said Fran. 'They organise Witch Wars. Why?'

Tiga's mind was racing. 'Whoever put me forward *knows* me. They know I exist and they think that I'm good enough to win Witch Wars. Maybe they can help me! I must go to Brollywood and find out who nominated me.'

Fran squealed. 'You will *love* Brollywood! Oh, and I can show you around! But first we have to begin Witch Wars.'

'OK,' Tiga said. 'I'm going to find the witch who nominated me. And I'm going to try to win Witch Wars! Anything to stay in Ritzy City. LET'S DO THIS, FRAN.' She marched over to the sofa and sat down confidently, only this time it didn't flip.

'It's a bit fiddly sometimes,' Fran mumbled, giving it a kick.

# Witch Wars
# Begins

Once the sofa had flipped back round, Tiga found the other girls near the front door, surrounded by a swarm of witches.

Peggy was grinning at a plump little woman with a sweet smile.

Felicity Bat was rolling her eyes. 'Mother,' she said, staring coldly at a wisp of a woman who stood in the shadows with her arms folded.

Next to her, a woman covered from head to toe and arm to arm in massive jewellery jumped and jingled in front of Aggie Hoof. 'Oh, my beautiful darling, you look wonderful in that very expensive hat. VERY EXPENSIVE.' She looked around the room for approval, but only Tiga was listening.

Meanwhile, Mrs Brew, in a very elaborate wide-brimmed hat with feathers and swirly bits of glass sticking out of it glided up to Fluffanora. 'Now, dear, remember this is a wonderful opportunity.' She straightened Fluffanora's hat and gave her a big hug.

Tiga watched Fluffanora squirm in her mother's arms. And then she looked to her left where Peggy was reluctantly dabbing a hanky under her sobbing mother's eyes. And over in the shadows Felicity Bat's mum was holding out a hand and sort of awkwardly patting her on the head. They all looked so irritated by each other, and Tiga wanted that too! She bit her lip and leaned against the bookcase.

That's when she saw it.

It practically fell off the bookshelf on to her foot. If 'falling off the bookshelf and on to her foot' actually meant 'sneakily pulling it out of the bookshelf'.

*Sinkville Spells, Potions and Cat Food Recipes.*

It was tiny and bound in flaky old leather. Tiny enough to fit in a witch's pocket …

'Fairy flattener,' Fran said, making Tiga jump. She held the book behind her back.

'Fairy flattener?' Tiga asked.

Fran nodded at Lizzie Beast's mum. She was huge and grinning a gigantic grin.

Mrs Brew walked over to Tiga and tapped her shoulder. 'I wish you lots of luck, Tiga,' she said, giving her a hug. 'I will cheer for you *and* Fluffanora!'

Tiga hugged her so tightly she thought she heard one of the glass swirls on her hat popping off.

'Oh, Mrs Brew, Mrs Brew, Mrs Brew!' Fran squealed.

Mrs Brew forced a smile and tried to step around the fairy.

'I'M WEARING ONE OF YOUR DRESSES, MRS BREW!'

'Yes,' Mrs Brew said with a kind smile. 'Very nice.'

'I WEAR YOUR DRESSES BECAUSE I LOVE YOU!' Fran roared.

Tiga laughed, but then she noticed the front door was creaking open. No one else seemed to notice. Tiga edged closer. As she reached for the handle, the door flew open.

'Genuine hats wots got stuck in the pipes! The genuine article! Get yer genuine hats from the pipes above!'

In the doorway stood an extremely grubby old witch. She had an old cart filled with the most disgustingly tattered and slimy hats.

Tiga didn't know, but the grubby old witch had been part of Witch Wars since the competition first began, over a thousand years ago. So really she looked very good for her age.

Fran clapped her hands. 'Right, it's time. Come along, out the door! Line up outside!'

It was a tradition that the old witch appeared outside Linden House before each competition to present the shrivelled heads and predict the winner. She had never been wrong – that's why she wore a badge that said, 'I AM NEVER WRONG.'

Fran raised her hands in the air. 'OK, old cart witch lady, the shrivelled heads!'

The witch cackled loudly.

*BANG!*

'What just happened?' Peggy said.

Tiga turned to look at her and there, right in her face, was a shrivelled Peggy head, nestled on the rim of Peggy's hat.

Peggy pointed at Tiga's and laughed.

'Ha! Tiga, your head!'

Tiga lifted her hat off and looked at her tiny shrivelled head. It looked all wrinkly and terrifying, and her eyes were closed.

Tiga spotted Fluffanora in the corner staring at her shrivelled head and gagging.

Fran clapped her hands and zoomed around above

the crowd, who were all pointing at the shrivelled heads and squealing.

'QUIET!' she bellowed.

The crowd fell silent.

She cleared her throat and said softly. 'And now old cart witch lady, tell us, *who* is going to win?'

The old witch stepped forward and, after a really long pause, croaked the following very important words:

'*An elegant witch will rule this land,*

*And that bossy one will lend a hand.*

*Witch sisters, maybe, but not the same.*

*One is dear.*

*The other? A PAIN.*

*And, much like the tales of times gone by,*

*They will find a sweet apple and …* My oh my, is that the time? I'd better go.'

And off she hobbled, pushing her creaky cart through the silent crowd. Once she'd got near the back she shouted, 'Real witch hats wot fell from the pipes!' and everyone jumped.

# Some Fairies

'Elegant?' Peggy said. 'Well, it's definitely not me.'

'Or you,' Felicity Bat said to Tiga.

'Oooh, I'm elegant, Fel-Fel,' said Aggie Hoof, hugging Felicity Bat's arm, 'and you're *really* bossy.'

'Yeah, but neither of you are dear. You're both pains,' said Fluffanora.

Fran shot some glittery dust at them and the conversation stopped. Almost all the glittery dust ended up in Peggy's mouth. She coughed and a clump of glitter fell out, like a dressed-up fur ball.

'I present each of you,' Fran said grandly, 'with a map, and the brilliant book, *The Not Nearly Complete History of Sinkville*, to help you on your way.'

In front of each witch, a rolled-up map and a dusty

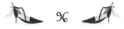

old book fell from above and landed with a thud.

Aggie Hoof picked up hers and tossed it to the side. 'I only read *Toad* magazine.'

Tiga flipped through the pages.

## THE YEAR OF SITTING DOWN

Everyone, at some point, during the Year of Sitting Down, sat down.

Tiga looked up from the book just as Fran shouted, 'OK! So now we begin the countdown!'

The crowd went wild!

'A-three! A-two! A–'

A woman holding a clipboard in the crowd hissed, 'Fairies.'

Tiga spotted a tiny bead of sweat fall from Fran's head.

'Ah, the f-fairies,' stuttered Fran. 'Oops, yes, almost forgot THE FAIRIES!' And, just like that, a bunch of

fairies fell from above and landed with a thud on the pavement. All eyes in the crowd shifted from the Witch Wars witches to the crumpled fairies on the ground.

'You will each be given a fairy to assist you, kindly provided by Brollywood Studios. The fairies will also film your activity for all of Sinkville to see, with the small cameras attached to their heads!'

The crowd cheered. Fran looked pleased with herself.

'Patty Pigeon, you will have Sally.'

The smallest fairy peeled herself off the pavement and glared at Fran. She flew into the air and zoomed around Patty Pigeon.

'Fluffanora, you have the lovely Millbug-Mae ...'

Millbug-Mae, a round little fairy with oversized eyeballs, flew over to Fluffanora and sat on her shoulder.

'Lizzie Beast, you have Julie Jumbo Wings.'

'IT'S JUST JULIE!' the fairy yelled. She stood up and flew elegantly through the air, one arm outstretched. Her wings, which were bigger than Tiga's hands, slapped against Peggy's face as she went.

'Ow. Nope. I'm fine! Just my face ...' Peggy said, rubbing her cheek.

Milly and Molly got a couple of fairies called the Sulky Sisters. They flew around saying, 'Ugh, hate this! Can't be bothered. Ugh, why us? Ugh.' And Felicity Bat got a fairy with fangs called Crispy. Tiga thought Crispy looked a lot like a fairy whose face had melted and someone had unsuccessfully tried to squash it back together. Aggie Hoof's fairy was far less scary, but she was having problems with her.

'Just FLY, Donna, *please*,' Aggie Hoof pleaded.

Donna the fairy threw her hands in the air. 'Oh right, so just because I'm a *fairy*, you think I should *fly*. Fly, little fairy, fly! You're so rude.'

Aggie Hoof got down on her hands and knees. 'But we're never going to get anywhere, Donna, if you *walk*!'

Donna scowled.

'Tiga, that just leaves you, and you, my dear, get me! Eek! How exciting for you!' Fran swirled around in front of her. Tiga wasn't sure if it was a good thing to be lumbered with Fran. She supposed she could've got slow-walking Donna or terrifying Crispy, but Fran was mad! Fabulous, yes. But also mad.

Tiga heard a cough behind her. It was Peggy.

'Oh, Peggy, the glitter will be completely out of your mouth soon. Be quiet,' Fran said impatiently before flashing the audience a big smile.

'Oh, no, sorry, Fran, I was doing the coughing thing to get your attention. You see, I haven't got a fairy.'

The woman in the crowd with the clipboard ran a finger down the page. 'Bow,' she yelled over to Fran.

'Ah, Bow, yes! Peggy's fairy.' Fran zoomed around for a bit and then shook her head. 'She's a no-show. No-show Bow.'

'What?' Peggy said.

'She's not showed up – she's not here – so you won't have a fairy, Peggy. You might not even be seen in Witch Wars. Sorry.'

Peggy raised a finger and opened her mouth to say something in protest, but there was a massive bang and some letters exploded in the air.

Peggy sighed.

'The first clue!' Fran said, zooming around the glittery letters.

> *If every witch in this city*
> *Sat on your shoulders,*
> *It wouldn't be pretty!*
> *A pile of you lot in a fuss*
> *Could never be as tall as us.*

The witches stared up at the clue.

'Huh?' said Aggie Hoof.

Fran wiggled in the air. 'Oh! Forgot the last bit!'

Some more glittery letters exploded in the air.

*In order to single me out from the rest,*
*Look for a shouting big, bald PEST.*

'Huh?' said Aggie Hoof.

'AND WITCH WARS IS A GO!' Fran yelled, before turning to Tiga and saying quickly, 'Felicity Bat is about to attack you.'

# The First
# Clue

It all happened very quickly. So quickly, in fact, that it has gone down in history as the quickest Witch Wars fight on record.

Felicity Bat flew towards Tiga, her arms outstretched and clearly aimed at the shrivelled head on top of Tiga's hat.

If it was viewed in slow motion, which it was by millions watching the replay on the Fairy Network, this is what happened:

Donna the fairy bit Aggie Hoof's toe; Aggie Hoof then spun round and knocked into Peggy, who fell forward and straight into Lizzie Beast, who turned to see what Peggy was doing, hit one of Julie's jumbo wings and sent her spinning through the air, straight into

Felicity Bat's face. Peggy realised what was going on, grabbed Tiga's arm, screamed, 'THIS WAY!' and – even though she had absolutely no idea where she was going – ducked down a side street and ran and ran, and ran quite a lot more.

'I think we've lost her,' Tiga said. 'Thanks, Pegs.'

'Do you mean Felicity Bat … or FRAN?' Peggy panted, struggling to speak.

'Er, I meant Felicity Bat, but, Peggy, we have also lost Fran …'

They looked up and down the street, and up in the air.

'We've definitely lost Fran,' Tiga concluded.

'Or *have* you?' Fran said, walking down the wall, looking smug. 'I'm a pro, you know. When I did a TV show about fairies who refuse to fly, called *Wasted Wings*, I ran around a lot, so let me tell you I'm well prepared for this competition.'

Peggy was still panting. She was doubled over now. She held up a hand. 'That's great, Fran.'

'That was close,' Tiga said nervously.

Peggy wheezed and pulled her notebook out of her pocket. She shakily scribbled the clue in it and placed it on the ground.

'I have no idea what that means,' she said.

They all crowded around it.

'It's something tall … Maybe it's a giant! They're much taller than a pile of witches,' suggested Tiga.

Peggy cackled. 'Giants aren't *real*!'

'Well then, maybe it's a mountain? What about that Pearl Peak place Aggie Hoof was harping on about?'

'It could be Pearl Peak, I suppose,' mumbled Peggy, pulling the map out of her pocket. 'But no. The clue was "could never be as tall as *us*". There's only one mountain. It must be a group of tall things.'

Tiga's eyes darted about the map and settled on a cluster of really tall, spindly buildings. They were the tallest things on the map.

'*The Towers*,' she read.

'THE TOWERS!' Peggy cheered.

# Fluffanora Gets
# What She Wants

Meanwhile, back on the street about ten steps down the road from Linden House, Aggie Hoof was on her knees.

'PLEASE JUST *FLY*, DONNA! FLY! *PLEASE!*'

Nearby, Fluffanora was speaking to Mavis by the jam stalls.

'The thing I like most about jam is the word. *Jam*. It's a good word, isn't it?' Fluffanora said, turning a jar of jam in her hand. 'Jam. Jam. Jam. Jam.'

Mavis raised an eyebrow. 'Aren't you meant to be competing in Witch Wars, Fluffanora?'

Fluffanora shook her head. 'Not interested, Mavis. Not interested.'

Just then, the tattered old witch with the cart of hor-

106

rible hats creaked past. Fluffanora and Mavis watched her trundle on down the road towards Aggie Hoof.

'Genuine hats wot I got from the pipes! Genuine hats from the pipes! Who wants genuine hats from them pipes wot I got from up there?'

'DONNA, JUST FLY!'

Aggie Hoof wasn't paying attention at all. The old witch came to a halt next to her. 'Genuine hats wot I got from the pipes!'

'PLEEEEASE!' Aggie Hoof roared.

Well, the tattered old witch thought she meant 'PLEASE give me a hat!', which of course she didn't. And so she lifted off Aggie Hoof's hat and plonked a disgusting slimy one on top of her head.

'Ta da! Wots you got there, little witchy, is a genuine hat wot I got from the pipes above!'

There was a pause. Everyone on the street seemed to freeze, apart from Donna, who adjusted the tiny camera on her head and pointed it at Aggie Hoof.

'What … is … on … my *HEEEEEEEEEAD*?' Aggie Hoof screeched. Her voice shot up the street and

bounced off the buildings. Almost everyone within a mile radius heard her, including Tiga, Peggy and Fran, who were only a couple of streets away, racing towards the hillside where the tall towers stood.

Peggy skidded to a halt.

'What do you think just happened?' Tiga asked.

Peggy held Tiga's hand up. 'TV, TV, TV, TV, TV, TV,' she said.

An image appeared. It was Aggie Hoof spinning round madly. She was spinning so fast all they could see was a huge puffy dress and a bit of hair sticking out the top. And on top of that hair was a crusty old pointed hat.

'GET IT OFF! GET IT OFF MY HEAD!'

'Oh, calm down,' Fluffanora said, strolling over. But Aggie Hoof couldn't hear anything over her own screeching, and she certainly couldn't see anything from under the hat.

'Let me just take –' Fluffanora began. But, before she could finish, Aggie Hoof spun and smacked into her.

Fluffanora's hat flew off.

Aggie Hoof continued to spin round madly.

'TAKE IT OFF, TAKE IT OFF!'

Fluffanora did just that. She lifted the hat off Aggie Hoof's head.

'Oh, Fluffanora!' she squealed. 'I knew we would be friends! You saved me!' She took a step forward to try to hug Fluffanora.

*CRUNCH.*

Aggie Hoof stared down at her feet and her mouth fell open.

'YOU SILLY NONSENSE STUPID RUBBISH FROGFACE IDIOT!' roared Millbug-Mae, pointing a tiny finger at Aggie Hoof. It was the first thing Millbug-Mae had said, and it was an interesting choice of words …

'Aggie Hoof just squashed Fluffanora's shrivelled head!' Peggy cried.

Tiga stared at the TV screen. Black smoke was billowing up Fluffanora's legs.

Aggie Hoof slowly backed away, and then shot off down the street. Donna the fairy sat down cross-legged on the pavement and waved as the irritating witch disappeared into the distance.

Tiga watched in horror as the black smoke engulfed Fluffanora and she disappeared with a little pop.

Fran giggled like a lunatic and pointed at the screen. 'Oh, I love the pop! Before it was just smoke and disappearing. *I* suggested adding the pop. It really adds something, doesn't it?'

'Where did she go?' Tiga asked.

'She's *fine*. She's been sent home,' said Fran.

Behind them, a little further down the road back at Linden House, the flag with Fluffanora's face on it curled up and fell to the ground.

# FLUFFANORA IS OUT!

The daughter of Ritzy City's most famous designer is the first to be knocked out of the competition, less than an hour after it began! Our reporter caught up with Fluffanora to ask her some questions.

**Reporter:** You're out, Fluffanora. How do you feel?

**Fluffanora:** Yeah, good, thanks.

**Reporter:** How do you feel about the fact Aggie Hoof, Pearl Peak's richest kid and owner of Sinkville's only diamond-covered pet octopus, was the one who knocked your shrivelled head off? Fluffanora ... ?

NOTE FROM THE *RITZY CITY POST* EDITOR: THIS INTERVIEW ENDED ABRUPTLY AS FLUFFANORA WENT INSIDE CLUTTERBUCKS AND OUR REPORTER WASN'T ALLOWED IN.

And so, a final word from Fluffanora's fairy Millbug-May.

**Millbug-May:** END! That's a final word, isn't it?

**Reporter:** Oh, never mind.

# Felicity Bat Is Evil, But Also Clever

'Oh, I'm such a beautiful idiot!' Aggie Hoof cried, clutching the copy of the *Ritzy City Post*, which had only seconds earlier been shot out of a cannon. 'I can't believe I crushed her shrivelled head.'

'I know,' Felicity Bat said. 'It was brilliant.'

Aggie Hoof's eyes widened. 'Was it, Fel-Fel?'

Felicity Bat wasn't really listening; she was busy scrunching up the bed covers in Linden House with her hands. Well, she was scrunching her hands in the air and the bed covers were moving.

'And now, Crispy, you point your little camera here.'

Terrifying Crispy waddled over to the edge of the bed and pointed her camera at the lump of covers.

'Fel-Fel, what are you doing … ?'

Felicity Bat took the hat off her head and placed it on top of the covers. 'Excellent.'

Aggie Hoof raised a finger in the air. 'Ah! I see what you're doing! You're going to pretend it's you in bed and then you're going to make Crispy stand here all day long, videoing it!'

'That way,' Felicity Bat said smugly, 'no one will know where I am.'

Crispy flung her arms in the air. 'I DON'T WANT TO STAY HERE!'

Felicity Bat only looked at the fairy, but the look was enough to terrify Crispy.

'OK, I'll stay right here,' she said obediently.

Felicity Bat marched out of the door with Aggie Hoof trotting along at her side.

'Give me that hat,' Felicity Bat snapped, grabbing the hat off Aggie Hoof's head.

'But now I don't have a hat!' Aggie Hoof cried.

'Be quiet,' Felicity Bat snapped.

'Yes, Fel-Fel.'

# The Towers

Over at the Towers, there were towers EVERY-WHERE. On top of the hill, down the side of the hill – there were even a couple of pointy roofs sticking out from the ground, so Tiga assumed there must be towers *in* the hill as well.

Some were built with black bricks, others with black marble; one was built with black stones and some were built with black wood. Most were tall and narrow with all sorts of roofs, some swirled like the top of an ice cream cornet, and some had flat roofs like the top of an ice cream that someone had jumped on.

'We're never going to find the right tower! There are *hundreds* of them!' Tiga cried. 'What did the clue say?'

'We need to look for a shouting big, bald pest,' Peggy said with a shrug.

They weaved in and out of the towers, listening for shouts and looking for something bald.

Each door had a number, but underneath, in tiny letters, there were also words. At first Tiga thought they were the names of the people who lived inside, but when she got closer she realised it wasn't that at all.

THE CUPBOARD IN CAKES, PIES AND THAT'S ABOUT IT REALLY.

'Um, Fran, why is this sign on the door?' Tiga asked. She knew Cakes, Pies and That's About It Really was all the way back in town, near Linden House.

'It's a shortcut, dear,' said Fran.

'Don't you have shortcuts in the world above the pipes?' Peggy asked.

'Well, yes,' said Tiga. 'But a shortcut above the pipes is something like a road that is quicker than another road, not a tower on a hill.'

Fran twirled in the air. 'Well, here at the Towers each tower is a shortcut to somewhere else. So the witches

who live in them live on the second floor and any other floors above that, and on the ground floor is a hole. That hole is a shortcut to somewhere else. When a witch buys a tower, she gets to pick where she wants her shortcut to go. These witches obviously like cakes and pies and That's About It Really tarts!'

Tiga ran from tower to tower looking at all the signs. PEARL PEAK BOOKSHOP, CLUTTERBUCKS (MEMBERS ONLY), THE GULL AND CHIP TAVERN, BROLLYWOOD PRODUCTION STUDIOS …

She stopped and stared up at one of them. NO.17 BROLLYWOOD PRODUCTION STUDIOS.

Brollywood.

The place where someone knew who had put her forward for Witch Wars. Brollywood …

'Ah, Brollywood!' Fran said. '*Home.*'

Tiga reached for the handle. 'I think we should check Brollywood for a clue.'

'Brollywood?' Peggy asked, sounding confused. 'That's not what the clue said.'

'I know,' said Tiga. 'I mean a clue about who put

me forward for Witch Wars. Fran said they know in Brollywood.'

Peggy stared at Fran.

'They *might* know,' Fran said.

'Well, we could go. It might make us fall behind in the competition, but I know it's important to you …' Peggy muttered.

Tiga jumped up and down. 'Thank you, Peggy!'

Something fell out of Tiga's pocket.

'Tiga,' Peggy said, bending down to pick it up. 'You dropped *Sinkville Spells, Potions and Cat Food Recipes*! Where did you find this?'

Tiga grabbed the book. 'I borrowed it from Linden House, to help.'

Peggy nodded. 'Let's see if there is a spell to help us find the right tower! *Then* we can go to Brollywood.'

Tiga reluctantly opened it. It was ninety per cent cat food recipes.

'Um …' she said, flicking through the pages. 'What about … ?'

Fran zoomed around her head. 'That won't work.

Not that one. The last thing you want is to make the towers invisible! No, that one will make everything explode …'

'WHAT ABOUT THIS?' Tiga cried, pointing at a spell called 'Highlight'. 'This spell will highlight what you're looking for,' she read.

'Sounds good to me,' said Peggy, standing back as Tiga shouted, 'High-light, high-light, make the answer outrageously bright!'

An obscenely bright light waved about madly on top of one of the towers.

'The others will see that too and know which tower it is now, won't they?' Tiga said, shaking her head.

Peggy wrinkled her nose. 'Um, probably, yup. It's not ideal BUT YOU DID A SPELL! Well done.'

Tiga felt like a complete failure and a genius all at once.

They scuttled around the towers and reached the glowing one.

'CLIMB UP MY SILKY BLACK HAIR! CLIMB UP THE HAIR!' shouted a very bald witch high up in the tower.

# Hair

'THE HAIR, DEARS! CLIMB IT!' the bald witch cried.

'Um,' Peggy said, shifting from foot to foot. 'You … don't … have any?'

'I don't think she knows she's bald,' Tiga whispered.

'CLIMB THE SILKY HAIR TO REACH THE SHORTCUT!'

Tiga looked at the tower door – it wasn't like the others. Instead of a sign saying where the shortcut led to, this one had nothing.

'REACH THE SHORTCUT BY CLIMBING MY SILKY HAIR!'

Tiga and Peggy stared at her blankly.

'CLIMB MY SILKY HAIR!'

Peggy inched closer towards the door and twisted the handle and frowned. 'It's locked!' she hissed.

'DID YOU JUST TRY TO OPEN THE DOOR?' the witch bellowed. 'DID YOU JUST TRY TO GET INTO MY TOWER THROUGH THE *DOOR?* YOU WERE SUPPOSED TO CLIMB MY SILKY HAIR!'

'Maybe we could try a spell?' Tiga whispered.

'GOOD LUCK FINDING A SPELL THAT OPENS THAT DOOR! CLIMB UP MY SILKY HAIR!' the witch yelled.

The witch was yelling so loudly that Tiga almost didn't hear the footsteps.

'Is that –?' Peggy began.

'It's Molly and Milly!' Fran bellowed.

'Oh no, oh no, oh no, oh no, where do we hide?' Peggy said, leaping from foot to foot, and falling over again. She grabbed her hat and checked her shrivelled head. It was fine.

'This way!' Tiga yelled. They raced from tower to tower, to tower to tower, and straight through a door and down a shortcut.

'Funny we ended up falling down the Brollywood shortcut,' said Peggy with a smile.

'I know! How *weird*,' Tiga said unconvincingly. 'Well, we might as well look into who nominated me. Since we're here.'

# Interlude in Brollywood

'I AM SO EXCITED I GET TO SHOW YOU ALL OF BROLLYWOOD. BECAUSE WE MIGHT AS WELL SINCE WE'RE HERE AND EVERYTHING, AND OH! NOT FAR FROM HERE IS MY LITTLE MINI CARAVAN. You won't be able to sit in it because you're far too big. But I can *tell* you about it, oh yes!'

Fran was rambling like a mad fairy.

Peggy and Tiga were slumped on a chair, surrounded by costumes and hats and glasses and wigs and shoes, and there were some cars and a fake grey parrot sitting in an old bucket.

'We're in the prop cupboard. Although it's more of a large room than a cupboard,' Fran said.

'Which witch would know who nominated me?' Tiga asked.

'Why, the *Witch Wars* producer, of course!' said Fran.

Tiga leapt off the sofa. 'Then take me to the producer!'

Fran nodded. 'OK, but only if you call me fabulous!'

Peggy giggled.

'Fabulous Fran,' Tiga said with a sigh, 'please take me to the producer of *Witch Wars*.'

'Oh, you're too kind, Tiga!' Fran said. 'Now, grab an umbrella.'

Brollywood was exactly how Tiga imagined it would be from the map in Linden House. There were a lot more pipes hanging in the sky than there were in Ritzy City, which meant it was much, much wetter.

'They once did a hilarious programme about people who accidentally fall down the pipes in Brollywood!' Fran chuckled as she ducked and dived, trying to avoid the streams of water.

'Normal people, not witches?' Tiga asked.

Fran nodded. 'Occasionally it happens. Of course we send them straight back. I like to return them with a little memento – a framed and signed picture of my face, for example. You can buy them in there.' Fran was pointing at a small shop with hundreds and hundreds of pictures in the window, mostly of her. Next to it stood a big van filled to bursting with huge lights. And next to that was a shiny black building shaped like a castle.

'Patricia the producer works in there,' Fran said, nodding at the fake castle. 'Oh, here she is now!'

Tiga looked up and saw a witch soaring through the air holding an umbrella.

'She saw it in a film once and now it's the only way she'll travel,' Fran said, looking at the producer in awe.

'Supercallifrag– oh FROGBISCUITS!' Patricia cried as she crash-landed at Tiga's feet. She got up and straightened her gigantic glasses and tiny hat.

'Ah, hello. You'll not find any Witch Wars clues in Brollywood. I probably shouldn't tell you that …'

'Oh! So you know all the clues!' Peggy said. 'How can we get into the bald woman's tower?'

Patricia the producer cackled. 'Ha, I can't tell you that!'

'Who nominated me for Witch Wars?' Tiga asked, taking a step forward.

'Afraid I can't tell you that either – it's confidential,' Patricia the producer said, which was not what Tiga wanted to hear at all.

'But everyone else knows who nominated them! Peggy knows it was her gran; Fluffanora knows it was her mum!'

'Well, they aren't meant to tell,' Patricia the producer said, sounding a tad annoyed.

 128

Her walkie-talkie crackled. 'Oi, Patricia! They want you on set five. There's a fairy stuck in a melon.'

She sighed. 'We'll be happy to have you back on *Cooking for Tiny People* when Witch Wars is over, Fran. It's proving to be a bit of a disaster without you.'

Fran looked smug as Patricia walked away.

'Sorry they won't tell you,' Peggy said, turning and heading back to the prop cupboard. 'Shall we go and figure out how to get into the bald woman's tower?'

'Not yet,' Tiga said as she marched towards the fake castle.

# Felicity Bat
# Solves It

'You're bald,' Felicity Bat snapped. 'Stop shouting about your hair.'

'WHAT DID YOU SAY?' the bald woman cried.

'BALD,' Felicity Bat said impatiently.

Aggie Hoof was staring up at the woman, shaking her head. 'It makes me so sad to see a bald witch when I have such perfect hair.'

Felicity Bat ran at the door again.

'Fel-Fel, I don't think it's going to open.'

'Be quiet!' Felicity Bat snapped.

'CLIMB UP MY SILKY HAIR TO GET TO THE SHORTCUT!' the bald woman cried.

'OH, WILL YOU BE QUIET?' Felicity Bat bellowed.

'Maybe Piggy and that girl from above the pipes already got inside and locked it!'

'Unlikely,' Felicity Bat said, fiddling with the handle. 'Check on them.'

Aggie Hoof stared at one of the bricks on the tower and mumbled 'TV' a lot. A moving image appeared on the brick. It was Lizzie Beast walking along a path with Patty Pigeon.

'It's just showing that big lump of a witch walking along a path,' Aggie Hoof said.

But then the channel switched to an image of Peggy and Tiga surrounded by huge piles of paper. 'Where *are* they?'

Felicity Bat dropped the door handle she had just snapped off and stared intently at the brick.

'That's Brollywood – look at the water outside the window. They obviously got the first clue wrong.'

'Are you *sure*, Fel-Fel? *Toad* says you should never trust someone with frizzy hair and Piggy has the frizziest hair I've ever seen.'

Felicity Bat sighed. 'We're wasting time here. If this

irritating bald lady won't let us through the door, we'll just have to do it her way.'

'Her way?' Aggie Hoof asked as Felicity Bat levitated up and up until she was nose to nose with the bald witch. She grinned a menacing grin as the bald witch stumbled backwards.

# The Brollywood File

Papers soared through the air.

'It's not here!' Peggy said from the heap she was sitting on.

'I just want to say, I am *not* OK with this,' said Fran.

Tiga slumped in a comfy chair behind a massive black desk. They had emptied every filing cabinet in Patricia the producer's office.

'We aren't having much luck,' Tiga said, slamming her head down on the desk.

It was really lucky she did that, because as soon as she did a drawer in the desk shot out and hit her in the stomach.

'The Witch Wars files!' she squealed, pulling a clump

of papers out of the secret drawer. 'Peggy, I found them! I FOUND THEM!'

Peggy and Fran raced over.

'*Felicity Bat,*' Tiga read, '*recommended by Mrs Bat, Moira the Mean and Nasty Nancy.*'

'Felicity Bat knows all the bad witches in Sinkville,' Peggy said.

Tiga held the paper close to her face. It couldn't be right. All the others had names next to them. Peggy had her gran, Fluffanora had her mum, but Tiga didn't have a name. It just said, *Anonymous letter*.

'*A-n-o-n-y-m-o-u-s letter,*' Peggy read slowly.

Tiga pulled a letter from the pile.

*Tiga Whicabim for Witch Wars* was all that was written on it. She flipped it over and stared at it in disbelief.

'Do you recognise the writing?' Peggy asked.

Tiga shook her head. 'Is this A JOKE? They must know who sent it. It must be a mistake.'

'Oh, we don't make mistakes in Sinkville,' Peggy said. 'Sure, we once accidentally built a circus instead of a hospital, and there was that time we tried to wear jelly, but we never make mistakes when it comes to Witch Wars.'

Tiga stared at the letter, and all across Sinkville witches watched the footage from Fran's camera on the backs of their spoons and said, 'Ooooh.'

Patricia the producer, who had just finished fishing a fairy out of a melon, spotted the Witch Wars coverage and now knew that Tiga and Peggy had broken into her office.

'Get them,' she said to ten huge witch security guards.

# Huge Security Witches and Tiga's Brilliant Move

'Why are those witches so HUGE?' Peggy cried as she and Tiga raced as fast as their little witch legs would carry them. 'THEY ARE AT LEAST TEN TIMES TALLER THAN NORMAL WITCHES!'

Tiga didn't dare to look back – she just ran, her eyes fixed on the prop cupboard door. *Please open*, she thought as she flew at it. She tumbled through with Peggy and Fran close behind.

'I'M SO SORRY, PATRICIA! IT'S NOT ME, I HAVE TO FOLLOW THEM!' Fran yelled. 'DON'T JUDGE ME, PATRICIAAAAAAAA!'

Peggy dived for the hole in the floor, but Tiga stopped and raced to the back wall of the cupboard.

'*WHAT ARE YOU DOING?*' Peggy cried.

The rumble of massive shoes was getting louder and louder.

Tiga grabbed some things off the wall.

'DON'T *STEAL*!' Peggy shrieked as Tiga raced back, grabbed her arm and they jumped down the hole.

Tiga glanced back just in time to see the limbs of ten huge and angry witch guards squashed in the door frame.

'You took things from the cupboard! Why would you do that?' Peggy asked as they were spat out of the shortcut on to the tower floor.

Tiga held up a handful of black, grey and white wigs.

'Not just any old things.'

# Bald No
# More

'SILKY BLACK HAIR, CLIMB UP MY SILKY BLACK HAIR!'

Tiga took a step forward. 'Um, I'm afraid to inform you … you don't actually have any hair.'

'OH YES I *DO*.'

'You definitely don't,' said Peggy.

'But we,' Tiga said, holding up the wigs, 'have some hair for you.'

Tiga opened her book of spells, flicked past all the cat food recipes, and tapped a finger on a potion called 'Grow'.

Peggy took off her hat and carefully, so as not to accidentally crush the shrivelled head, laid it on the ground. 'For the potion.'

'I thought witches used cauldrons?' Tiga said.

Peggy shook her head. 'That was in the olden days. Now we use pots and pans. Or anything that can hold the ingredients. Who's going to lug a massive iron cauldron around with them?'

Tiga smiled and read out the ingredients.

'*Some hair.*'

Peggy plucked a hair off her head.

'*A drop of water.*'

Peggy shook some water off the leaves of a nearby bush.

'*A dragon's bone.*'

Peggy looked around. 'That one might be a problem. Let's improvise with … a tiny stone?'

'Will that work?' Tiga asked.

Peggy tossed the stone into the hat along with the wigs, and they waited.

The wigs started to wriggle like cats.

'Well, they're growing, but they aren't stopping!' Tiga cried, holding up the wigs that were getting longer and longer by the second.

She held them in the air and waved them. 'New hair for you!'

The old witch's eyes lit up. 'Ooooh, grey!'

Fran rolled her eyes, grabbed hold of the wig and lugged it up the tower to the witch. She plonked it on her head.

'What do you think?'

'LOVELY!' Tiga and Peggy said together.

The no-longer-bald witch let down her grey wig and Tiga grabbed hold of it, but she spotted something odd on the tower. On one of the bricks there was a little moving image. It was the TV spell Aggie Hoof had cast earlier.

'Pegs, look,' she said.

'Is that … ?' Peggy began.

Tiga nodded and pointed at the bottom of the screen. It said, *Felicity Bat*.

'Is she … ?' Peggy said.

Tiga nodded. It looked to her like Felicity

Bat was in bed all the way back in Linden House.

'She's miles behind!' Peggy cried. 'What on earth is she doing? Having a *nap*?'

Tiga stared at the image of the witch asleep in bed. 'Something isn't right.'

'We'll beat her at this rate!' Peggy said, grinning at the screen.

Tiga wasn't so sure. She began climbing the grey hair.

'OUCH! BE GENTLE!' the woman cried.

'Sorry!' Tiga called up to her.

'You know, Tiga, we're going to be so far ahead of Felicity Bat,' said Peggy.

Tiga looked down to smile at her, and that's when she saw it.

Two little figures scuttled past the tower.

'It's Milly and Molly!' Tiga yelled. 'Climb faster, Peggy!'

But it was too late. The twins had spotted them and were pulling at the witch's hair.

'I SAID BE GENTLE!' the witch cried. 'GENTLE!'

Milly and Molly cackled and tugged harder.

'Ugh, this is so not what I want to be doing right now, videoing this silly battle. Ugh!' the Sulky Sister fairies groaned as Molly scrambled up the hair.

Tiga swung the hair back and forth, trying desperately to knock Molly off.

Molly reached up and grabbed hold of Peggy's shoe. Peggy was frantically trying to wiggle free.

'OUCH! GET OFF MY SILKY GREY HAIR! OUCH! I'M NOT A SWING!' the witch yelled.

'Sorry!' Tiga said as she stopped swinging on the hair. There was a crunch and the hair hung limply below her. She froze. 'Peggy?' She was afraid to look down.

There was nothing but silence and a little bit of huffing from the old witch in the tower. 'I don't have all day,' she said, even though she definitely did.

'Oh, Molly, I'm sorry! Did I get your nose?' Tiga heard below her. 'I really didn't mean to …'

'PEGGY!' Tiga cried.

When she looked down, she could see Peggy hanging on by no more than three fingers.

Molly was standing on the ground looking furious. In one hand she was clutching her nose, and in the other was a smashed shrivelled head. Black smoke was billowing up her legs.

'Ugh, one out! Knew we didn't have winners,' one of the Sulky Sisters groaned. 'UGH, RUBBISH.'

Molly disappeared with a pop.

'Ah, the pop,' said Fran, rocking on her heels in the air. 'Did I tell you adding the pop was my idea?'

Tiga didn't answer. Her eyes were fixed on Milly. What was she going to do? Get angry? Try to get revenge on Tiga and Peggy for knocking her sister's shrivelled head off?

She was going to do none of those things.

'I'm not doing Witch Wars without Molly,' she said, throwing her shrivelled head to the ground and jumping on it. Black smoke started to billow up her legs.

'Ugh, she gave up. Ugh, quitters,' the Sulky Sister fairies moaned.

# MILLY AND MOLLY ARE OUT!

A s things begin to get hairy in the Witch Wars competition, Milly and Molly are the latest to have their shrivelled heads crushed. Our reporter met them at their Ritzy City home to talk about what it's like to be out of the competition.

**Molly:** Well, at least mine was crushed by Peggy. Milly squashed hers herself.

**Reporter:** I haven't asked a question yet ...

**Milly:** Why not?

**Reporter:** Well, I was going to –

**Molly:** Are you good at interviewing people?

**Reporter:** Oh yes, very good.

**Milly:** What do you like most about interviewing people?

**Reporter:** Well, lots of things really! It all started when I was a child ...

NOTE FROM THE *RITZY CITY POST* EDITOR: WE ARE NOT GOING TO PRINT THE REST OF THIS INTERVIEW BECAUSE IT'S JUST MILLY AND MOLLY INTERVIEWING OUR REPORTER, WHICH IS THE OPPOSITE OF WHAT WAS MEANT TO HAPPEN.

And so, a final word from Milly and Molly's fairies, the Sulky Sisters.

**The Sulky Sisters:** Ugh, being interviewed is so *boring.* Ugh, rubbish.

**Reporter:** Thank you.

# Shortcut!

'We're going to win!' Peggy yelled back to Tiga as the pair of them clattered down the spiral staircase in the bald witch's tower. On either side sat messy shelves crammed with dolls and books and shoes. There was a kitchen on the third floor – it was all black, apart from the cupboard handles, which were bright white. And the sitting room on the second floor was all different shades of grey with old spotty cushions and peeling wallpaper.

'SHORTCUT!' Peggy cried, jumping off the last step and pointing at the hole in the floor.

Tiga spotted that the handle on the inside of the door had fallen off.

Peggy saw her looking at it. 'Maybe that's why we couldn't get in.'

'Or maybe someone tried to break in when we were in Brollywood. Was the handle broken on the other side of the door when we got back from Brollywood?' Tiga asked.

Peggy shrugged. 'Does it matter? Felicity Bat is asleep in Linden House. Fluffanora, Milly and Molly are out, Aggie Hoof is probably complaining to someone about her fairy not working properly and, even if Lizzie Beast or Patty Pigeon tried to break in, that probably means they haven't figured out how to get to the short-cut yet. We're winning, Tiga! We're winning. And, best of all, we're beating Felicity Bat!'

But as they fell through the shortcut Tiga couldn't shake the feeling that something wasn't quite right.

# Desperate Dolls

'I know where we are!' said Peggy. 'This is Desperate Dolls, the oldest doll shop in all of Sinkville. They only sell second-hand dolls with missing eyes, burnt hair or no limbs ...'

It was the creepiest shop Tiga had ever seen and it was filled with old broken dolls.

'But where in Sinkville are we?' Tiga asked, staring out of the grubby window and taking it all in. 'This reminds me a lot of the neighbourhood where I live with Miss Heks.'

It was old, crumbling and peppered with houses that looked as if they had died. There was not a single witch on the street; only the occasional flicker of light through a holey curtain suggested people lived there.

'We're in the Docks – my part of town!' Peggy said. 'Look, that's where all the mouldy jam from Ritzy City goes to be made into cat food!'

Fran was flying around the room, her nostrils flared like a worried horse. Tiga got the impression it wasn't Fran's kind of place.

'ALL THIS PLACE NEEDS IS SOME GLITTERY DUST! THAT WILL MAKE IT BETTER!' she roared.

Peggy held up a hand to protest and Fran smacked right into it and fell to the ground.

'I'm fine,' she squeaked.

'It's … nice,' Tiga lied.

'Thanks!' Peggy said. 'Most people think it's horrible, but you can find good things about it, if you try really, really, *really* hard.'

'You're a good thing about it,' Tiga said.

Peggy did a little bow and then lowered her voice to a whisper. 'Old Miss Flint over there, who owns this place, isn't a good thing about it …'

Peggy was right. Old Miss Flint, owner of Desperate Dolls, wasn't nice at all.

'Excuse me,' Tiga said.

'I don't speak to witches from that vile place above the pipes – they're almost as bad as them lot from Ritzy City,' Miss Flint hissed, looking at Peggy but pointing at Tiga. 'I got no time for them. Worst thing I ever heard, letting above-the-pipes witches into Witch Wars. Shouldn't be allowed, that's what I say.'

'I think it's fair,' Tiga said, standing tall.

Miss Flint moved closer to her, her long, crooked nose wobbling.

'Miss Flint,' Peggy said, stepping between them. 'We're here on a mission. We're looking for the next Witch Wars clue, and the shortcut at the Towers led us here.'

'Sorry, can't help you,' Miss Flint said, resuming her position behind a huge desk. 'No clues in here.' She stuck a massive plastic foot on to a tiny doll. Tiga couldn't be sure, but she was almost positive she saw the doll frown.

Fran sat on the desk, eyeing the doll suspiciously.

'Good as new,' Miss Flint said, standing the doll up. It had one tiny foot and one huge one, so it just wobbled and fell over.

Without taking her eyes off Miss Flint, Tiga slowly stepped backwards and made her way over to the shelves on the back wall. There were hundreds of head-less, limbless and burnt dolls crammed into every spare space. Tiga was almost positive she heard whispering as she passed the other shelves. She stopped and shook her head.

*Don't be silly, Tiga*, she thought. *They're just dolls.*

'So you weren't given a clue to give to the Witch Wars witches?' Tiga heard Peggy ask Miss Flint.

'Nope,' said Miss Flint, just as Tiga spotted something. On one of the shelves up high was a small doll with one eye missing and matted hair. But that's not all Tiga could see. There was some swirly writing scrawled on the bottom of its bare feet.

*Witch Wars. Witch Wars. Witch Wars. Witch Wars. Witch Wars* it read, which convinced Tiga it definitely had something to do with Witch Wars.

Slowly, she lifted the doll off the shelf. The other eye fell out, and as she bent down to pick it up a chorus of whispers echoed throughout the shop. Whispers that were coming from the dolls.

*'Rusted and old by the barnacles and stone,*
*There sits an old woman and a younger wee crone.*
*One rocks in her chair; one brushes her hair.*
*It's been three thousand years they've been sitting in*
*    there.'*

'*PEHHHHGGGGGGGGY!*' Tiga cried, racing to the front of the shop.

'Oh frogs,' Miss Flint grumbled.

'Pegs, did you hear that?'

Peggy looked confused.

'The whispering, Peggy!'

Peggy looked around the room. 'The whispering?'

Tiga turned to Miss Flint. 'They whispered the clue, didn't they?'

But Miss Flint just whistled as she stuck some fingers on to another doll.

'The dolls?' Peggy asked.

'I heard them!' said Fran, but no one was listening.

'Yes!' Tiga cried. And that's when she had the crushing realisation she'd completely forgotten all the words. 'Um, something about barnacles? Two women?'

Peggy stared at her blankly.

'Oh, something about three thousand years?'

Peggy took out her notebook and wrote down the snippets of clues. She bit the end of her pen. 'This could be anything.'

Tiga took out her map. 'Barnacles,' she said. 'They will be in or near water.' She studied the map and finally rested a finger on the murky water by the Docks. 'All the other water bits on the map are smooth or ponds, but this bit near the Docks is all rocky. Perfect for barnacles!'

Peggy was still biting her pen.

'Peggy?' Tiga said.

Peggy mumbled and continued to stare at the clues. Then she leapt in the air. 'THE COVE WOMEN!' she roared, grabbing Tiga's arm and dragging her out of the shop. '*It must mean the Cove women!*'

# Boats

Peggy stood on the edge of the dock, her dress billowing in the wind, which Tiga thought made her look like a little witch-pirate.

News had spread that there were Witch Wars witches at the Docks, and so everyone had thrown back their holey curtains, clambered out of their windows and assembled themselves in prime viewing position behind Tiga and Peggy. The hiss of excited whispers was putting Tiga off, but Peggy was focused on the Coves.

'So, that's them,' she said, pointing across the water to some dark, crumbling coves that stood on the other side looking cold and mean and … cove-ish.

'There's a story they tell here at the Docks,' said Peggy. 'Legend has it two old and incredibly evil witches

155

live in the Coves. The oldest witches in all of Sinkville. No one alive has ever seen them and any witch who has travelled into their dark and dangerous cove has never returned.'

'*WHAT?*' Tiga cried. 'Let's not go into the dark and dangerous Coves, then.'

Peggy held up *The Not Nearly Complete History of Sinkville* book. Under the heading *Dock Legends* was a drawing of two women. One was sitting in a rocking chair and one was brushing her hair.

Tiga knew the dolls had whispered something about one of the witches brushing her hair and one being in a chair, but she didn't want to tell Peggy.

'Didn't they say something about a rocking chair and brushing –' Fran began. Tiga whipped her hat off and covered the fairy with it.

'This sounds like the clue,' Peggy said, and her eyes followed Tiga's hat as it shuffled across the ground.

'Ignore that,' said Tiga.

Peggy pointed at the Coves. 'We have to go.'

'Not the creepy Coves, please …'

Peggy smiled. 'Come on, Tiga. It might be fun.'

'Well, how would we even get there? Where are the boats?' She looked around the docks. There were none to be seen.

'Boats?' Peggy said. 'Oh, right, *boats*! There don't seem to be any left. We'll have to swim.'

'We can't swim, Peggy,' Tiga said, grabbing her arm. 'It's too far. And my dress – it's from *Brew's*.'

Peggy stared at her. Tiga sensed it was a FOR FROGSTICKS, ARE YOU BEING SERIOUS? stare, but that didn't stop her.

'The lace, Peggy. It might … snag … on a rock or … a fish might nibble it …'

Peggy raised an eyebrow. 'Oh, sorry, *Aggie Hoof*, I didn't realise that dress was so important to you.'

Tiga realised she was going to have to do it. 'Oh, OK, you're right!' she said, and she plunged into the murky water.

'Did you say boat?' someone croaked.

An old witch appeared beside Peggy with a little rowing boat.

'Oh, Tiga! Look at that! There are some boats around here! My mistake! That's lucky because, now that I actually *look* at the Coves, it's much too far to swim. Yes, thank you old croaky witch lady, we will take that boat …'

# The Cove
# Witches

Peggy was rowing enthusiastically, like an excited pirate on fast-forward. Tiga was wringing the water out of her dress and glaring at her, and Fran was in a huff on the handle of the oar.

'This is terrifying!' Peggy said brightly.

Fran shook her head at Tiga. 'Pfft. Hiding me under a hat. It's almost as bad as swatting!'

Tiga turned round slowly in her seat. The Coves were looming over them now and in the distance she could just make out two small lights. They were coming from two little windows, which belonged to two long, thin turrets that sat at either end of a rambling old house. All the other windows were dark, and only a small trail of smoke snaked up from

the chimney, fading into the darkness that enveloped the place.

The boat crunched into the shimmering black rocks that lined the cove.

Peggy leapt out. 'This is so terrifying!'

'*This is so terrifying, this is so terrifying, this is so terrifying, this is so terrifying …*' echoed the Coves.

'Echo!' Peggy yelled.

'*Echo, echo, echo, echo, echo …*' went the echo.

'Hello, echo!' Peggy squealed, clearly enjoying herself.

Tiga had read enough books to know that this was the bit when instead of saying '*Hello, echo*' back, the echo would say something creepy like, '*Hello, Peggy … Hello, Peggy … Hello, Peggy.*'

But it didn't. Instead the door to the house swung open and an old witch with frazzled grey hair poked her head out.

'No one called Echo lives here. Go away!'

Peggy and Tiga jumped. Fran dived on to the rim of Tiga's hat and curled it over herself to hide.

'W-w-we're l-l-looking for –' Peggy stuttered.

'The Cove witches,' Tiga said, taking off her hat and shaking Fran off it.

The witch raised an eyebrow. 'Eh?'

'We're looking … for … the Cove witches,' Tiga said again, more shakily.

The witch stepped out from behind the door. She was wearing a beautifully structured black gown covered in huge silk roses. 'You are both witches, correct?'

Tiga and Peggy nodded.

'And you are standing in the Coves, correct?'

Tiga and Peggy nodded.

'So perhaps *you* are the Cove witches,' the witch said.

Tiga and Peggy looked at each other.

'But we just got here!' Peggy cried. 'And we've never been here before, so we can't be, because people have been talking about the cove witches for centuries!'

The witch smiled a warm smile. Well, as warm a smile as you can get when you have no teeth. 'Clever girl,' she said.

'I'm not,' Peggy said matter-of-factly. 'I'm *known* for not being clever.'

'Who says?' the witch asked.

'Everyone,' said Peggy glumly.

'Well, I do not know Everyone. But, whoever she is, she is very wrong.'

Peggy smiled. Tiga thought that was lovely of the witch and she seemed very nice, but she was a witch who was standing in a cove that no one had ever returned from, so …

Just then another head popped out from behind the door. She was a much younger-looking witch. She had sleek black hair twisted into a pretty bun and was wearing huge sunglasses, even though it was very dark.

'Visitors!' she squealed, leaping out from behind the door. She had a Brew's dress, Tiga was sure of it – a simple black silk design that fell just below her knees.

'Oh, we do enjoy visitors!' she said, rubbing her arms. 'It's cold out here tonight. I'm Bettie and this is Lily. Do come in out of the cold.'

'Yes,' said Lily. 'Do … come in … out of the cold.'

Tiga looked at Peggy. Peggy looked at the witches and shrugged her shoulders. Much to Tiga's horror, she started walking towards the house!

Fran rolled her eyes. 'Walking disaster that one.'

'Um, Pegs …' said Tiga.

But it was too late. Peggy was already inside the door.

# Cove
# Madness

Behind the door of the house in the cove lay a long, dark corridor lined with old paintings of even older-looking cakes. Tiga also spotted one of a fat cat juggling.

At the end of the corridor was a large door, its edges glowing from the light behind it.

'Isn't this fun?' Bettie said, skipping along arm-in-arm with Peggy. Tiga was walking nervously behind, next to a slow and shuffling Lily. She held on to her hat.

'Watch your head,' she whispered to Peggy, but she wasn't listening.

Up ahead, Bettie grabbed the handle and flung the door open. Light cascaded down the hall, wiping out the darkness. And when Tiga saw what lay beyond it she gasped.

'Wheeeeeeeee!' squealed a witch as she swung from a chandelier and landed with a thud on the table beneath. She grabbed a bottle and yanked the cork out with her jagged teeth. Another woman was stirring some chocolate in a bowl, next to five witches who were singing songs and cackling loudly.

The room was crammed with witches, and Tiga could see beyond into the next room and through to the next one after that – all of them were filled with witches, laughing and joking and having a whale-sized dolphin of a time. Or something like that.

'No one ever wants to leave!' Bettie laughed. 'We haven't been able to get rid of anyone for over three thousand years.'

'Life is one big party!' a witch on rollerblades squeaked as she skated past them and fell face-first on a cake. Uproarious laughter filled the room.

'This is Tiga and Peggy,' Lily announced to the room as she took a seat on a rocking chair in the corner.

'I don't remember telling her our names,' Tiga whispered to Peggy. 'Do you?'

'WITCH WARS WITCHES!' another witch cried as she danced past.

'Ah,' Tiga said. She'd forgotten witches all over Sink-ville were watching footage of her on *Witch Wars*.

Peggy wasn't listening anyway. She was grinning at a large witch floating fast up from her seat towards the ceiling. Her head crashed through the roof. She giggled and fell to the floor with a bang. Another witch's face appeared in the hole. 'Come upstairs!' she cried. 'We're having a party!'

'I can see why no one wants to leave!' Tiga said.

166

'We keep having to build more house to accommodate them,' said Lily, sighing at the hole in the roof. A sparkly shoe fell through it and landed on the table. 'I wish I'd never invented that levitation spell.'

'You invented the levitation spell?' Peggy asked, clearly impressed. 'That was you?'

Lily smiled. 'Completely by accident.'

Tiga watched as Peggy's mouth fell open. 'By accident? "LETTIE. MANTERRY. LIE. MOOD. LOBARLY. MAKE. MAH. MINS. SOUT" was by accident?'

Peggy's eyes shot to her feet. She frowned. No levitation.

Lily nodded. 'We were having a party, and we'd made lots of cakes and the bins were overflowing with bottles and old cake, and I said to Bettie, "Bettie Cranberry, I should probably take the bins out." But my voice was a bit muffled from all the cake in my mouth, so it came out as "LETTIE. MANTERRY. LIE. MOOD. LOBARLY. MAKE. MAH. MINS. SOUT", and then I just started floating!'

Tiga looked at Peggy, who was prodding Lily as if she was some sort of fascinating beast.

'You invented the levitation spell – one of the most difficult spells of all time – by *accident*? Tiga, she invented the levitation spell, by *ACCIDENT*!'

Tiga nodded. Perhaps she would've been more excited if she hadn't just learned the day before that levitation was a thing, and she wasn't still worried that the witches in the cove might eat them.

Tiga pointed at a painting of a woman in a gigantic ruffled skirt. 'Who's *that*?'

168

'Why, that's Eddy Eggby, fashion explorer!' Bettie said. 'She was brilliant. Disappeared about a hundred years ago. No one knows what happened to her.' She climbed up a bookcase and pulled a little leather folder down from the top shelf. 'She went on adventures above the pipes and brought back drawings of all the latest fashions. Fascinating stuff.'

Tiga took the folder and flicked through the papers. There were hundreds of little pencil drawings of women and scribbles next to them.

## Eddy Eggby's Fashion Findings from the Faraway Land Above the Pipes

### The Hobble Skirt
A most peculiar invention! The bottom of the skirt is so tight round the ankles that the women can barely walk and instead waddle like well-dressed penguins.

## Bonnets

The women are now wearing the same hats as babies! At first I feared giant babies had taken over the world. But it's just women in bonnets.

## Ruffle Bottoms

The fashion is all of a sudden nothing but ruffles on the bottom! It makes the wearer look as if they have sat in a cake and the cake has in turn stuck to the bottom. Quite extraordinary. I am a fan.

'Fluffanora would LOVE this!' said Tiga. 'She was fascinated by my jeans.'

'Take it!' said Bettie. 'We've all read it here.'

Tiga beamed. 'Thank you!'

'So you're from above the pipes, Tiga,' Lily said. 'What do you think of Sinkville?'

'It's incredible,' Tiga said. Then she realised something. 'You've lived here for thousands of years, haven't you?'

'I believe so,' said Lily.

'Do you know anyone who knows me?'

Lily got up off her chair and walked towards Tiga. 'Remind me of your surname.'

'Whicabim,' Tiga said, taking the anonymous letter out of her pocket.

'ANYONE KNOW A WHICABIM?' Lily roared.

There was a silence, followed by a chorus of 'NO!'

'Why do you want to know?' Lily asked.

'No reason,' Tiga said, and she stuffed the letter back in her pocket.

Peggy came racing into the room with cake all over her face.

'I fell into it,' she said, pointing at her chin.

Tiga hadn't even realised Peggy had left her side.

'AH, YOU'RE A GREAT GIRL!' a witch said, squeezing Peggy and shoving more cake in her face. 'ONE OF US!'

Between munches of cake, she managed to say, 'Tiga, I think I've found the next clue, but we have a problem.'

# The Clue?

On the wall, in a frame, there was absolutely nothing.

Above it was swirly Witch Wars writing that read, *Congratulations! You're the same distance from the beginning as you are from the end! Otherwise known as HALFWAY THERE. Well done.*

'The clue's been stolen!' said Tiga in despair.

All the witches nodded.

'The Bat girl,' one said. 'I told her not to do it!'

Tiga and Peggy slowly turned around.

'Felicity Bat?' Peggy asked.

'Yes,' said Lily, 'and her friend, Hoof. They left moments after you arrived. You just missed them.'

'But, wait,' Peggy said, sounding worried. She yelled,

'TV, TV, TV, TV, TV, TV!' at her hand. 'According to this, Felicity Bat is still asleep in Linden House.'

The camera was at a funny angle. Crispy had fallen asleep.

'She's such a mean cheat!' Tiga cried. Crispy isn't with her! Look, that's just scrunched-up covers and a hat!'

Fran was speaking frantically into a tiny phone. 'Patricia, something has gone wrong with the footage of Felicity Bat. It says she's in bed at Linden House, but she was just at the Coves by the Docks … OK, yes … yes, I would send Crispy to find Felicity at once. You should probably yell at Crispy too. Yes, YELL. And why is there no footage of Aggie Hoof? Ah, Donna is refusing to participate and is now getting her hair done? What is Donna getting done to her hair? No, you're right, that's not important.'

'Can you tell us the clue?' Tiga asked the witches.

They all shook their heads and carried on partying.

# The Clue

Felicity Bat took the little piece of paper out of her pocket.

> *I see most things in circles,*
> *At times the wrong way round,*
> *But why is it I never lose track*
> *Of where it is I'm bound?*

She smirked, ripped the piece of paper into little pieces and flung it into the murky grey water.

Aggie Hoof squealed and leapt on to Felicity's back as she levitated high up in the air. As they soared across the water, cackling as they went, Felicity Bat looked back and flicked her finger.

Over in the corner of the cove, the little rowing boat slid out into the water and sank.

# The Boat with the Feet

'Do you think someone took it?' Tiga asked.

Peggy was pacing back and forth by the edge of the water. Her fist was in her mouth. She shook her head in disbelief.

'Do you think Felicity Bat did this?' Tiga went on. 'Or did we just forget to tie it up?'

Peggy stopped and took her fist out of her mouth. 'There is a strong chance I didn't tie it up, but I'm going to assume it was definitely Felicity Bat.'

'OK …'

Peggy sat down on the ground and curled up in a little ball. 'We're stranded.'

'What?' Tiga asked.

'STRANDED.'

Tiga looked around the cove. There wasn't anything on which to float back across, and that made her realise something. 'Hey, Pegs … There wasn't anything else in this cove when we arrived, was there? No boat or anything?'

Peggy shook her head.

'Well, if Felicity Bat and Aggie Hoof were just in front of us, we would've seen their boat. But there was no boat on the water, and no boat in the cove, so how did they get here, and how did they get back?'

'Magic, probably,' Peggy said with a sigh.

'So … don't you think *we* could use magic to get back?'

Peggy got to her feet and walked over to Tiga. 'I've told you, I'm rubbish at all spells, especially complicated spells with weird words like the levitation one, which is what we would need to get across the water. Felicity Bat is brilliant at spells. She wins the GAS award at school all the time.'

'GAS,' Tiga said with a smile.

'Good at Spells. GAS,' Fran mumbled. She was half

asleep on the brim of Tiga's hat, curled up round the shrivelled head. Now that they were losing, Fran wasn't that interested any more.

'ARE YOU TWO STILL HERE?' came a voice from the far window.

'YES!' Tiga cried. 'Our boat is missing!'

'TAKE THIS!' There was a cackle as a large object fell from the window and landed with a thud on the ground. It was a large, black four-poster bed.

Tiga sighed. 'Great, what are we going to do with *that*?' She turned round to check Peggy wasn't crying, but Peggy was leaping from foot to foot.

'Oh, oh, oh, oh, oh! I can do something with that!'

And that's why if anyone in the Docks had peeked out of their holey curtains that evening, they would've seen Tiga and Peggy sailing across the water in a four-poster bed.

Well, more sinking than sailing.

'I'm not sure the feet are working!' Tiga cried.

Peggy had jumped on to the bed and muttered a short spell from Tiga's book: 'Take this land thing and make it be, a splashing and swimming THING OF THE SEA!' And then a row of about eight fat feet had appeared along the bottom of each side of the bed.

It wasn't ideal.

They were human feet and the toenails were painted with stripy nail polish. They slapped about madly in the water not really doing much. Tiga moved closer to the middle of the bed as the water sploshed up the sides and soaked the black blanket on which she was sitting. Fran was snoring on Tiga's hat and missing it all.

'I think there's a small chance we might be sinking!' Peggy yelled as she peered over the edge. She was hanging from one of the posts. Tiga decided to join her and climbed up. But, as she did, she noticed something strange. There were small lights dotted around, deep under the water.

'We might have to try to swim for it. This isn't good …' Peggy said. She flicked her finger, and the feet

started to splash more, but it was no good – they just seemed to speed up the sinking.

'Ah, frogfingers!' Peggy said.

Tiga had her eyes fixed on the lights below the water. She lifted off her hat, being careful not to shake Fran awake, and pulled the rolled-up map out from under it.

*I knew it!* she thought as she studied it. The Underwater World was right beneath them.

'WE'RE GOING DOWN!' Peggy said, holding her nose. 'Do you want to swim? I think it's that or die …'

Tiga quickly rolled up the map and stuffed it back in her hat. 'Hold on to the bedpost, Peggy, until we sink to the bottom.'

'What?'

Tiga nodded towards the lights that lay deep below. 'We'll go to the Sunken Ship Road Spa.'

Peggy was now up to her neck in water. 'THE WHAT?'

'You've never been to the Underwater World below the Docks?'

As Peggy's head went under, all Tiga could make out from the gurgles was something that sounded a lot like, 'THERE'S AN UNDERWATER WORLD BELOW THE DOCKS?'

# The Sunken Ship
# Road Spa

As the four-poster bed sank, and the bubbles from Peggy's and Tiga's mouths danced their way back up towards the surface, Fran zoomed around ranting.

'Oh, you woke me up! This is silly! You don't have a plan! You don't have the next clue! And you don't have time for this!'

Tiga was wondering how on earth Fran could talk perfectly normally whilst underwater.

'Well, what do you have to say for yourself?'

Tiga just widened her eyes and puffed out her cheeks, hoping Fran would notice she couldn't answer.

'Ooooooh, I've heard about this place,' Fran said, suddenly distracted. She pointed below her. 'They invite famous people like me here all the time. Oh, they'll be

excited to see me, I bet! I hope people don't crowd around and take pictures – that's always embarrassing!'

Tiga could see the lights more clearly now. There were chandeliers inside what looked like huge pristine glass boxes. Littered around outside them were hundreds and hundreds of old sunken boats. A small door on one of the glass boxes opened as they hit the bottom. In the doorway stood a witch. Her arms were folded. She was wearing what looked like a black jumpsuit and her hat, although it had a wide brim, was almost completely flat.

She nodded at them.

Tiga and Peggy let go of the bedposts and swam towards the glass box. As soon as they passed through the doorway, the water disappeared. Tiga took a huge breath. Peggy spat out some water on the floor. The woman looked disgusted.

'Sorry,' Peggy said, wiping her mouth.

Fran zoomed up to the witch. 'I'm Fran from the Fairy Network and these are Witch Wars witches, Tiga and Peggy.'

'Ah, yes, Witch Wars. One of our best clients is owned by a Witch Wars witch.' She pointed at a picture on the wall of a smug-looking octopus covered in diamonds. 'Olive the octopus, owned by Aggie Hoof. She comes in here to get her diamond tentacles polished every week.'

Tiga giggled and nudged Peggy. The spa witch ushered them down the hall. 'Welcome to the Sunken Ship Road Spa. Here on Sunken Ship Road we do spa treatments better than anyone.'

'Ooh, I've heard that,' Fran said, wriggling with excitement.

'What treatments would you like today? We have some specials at the moment. Our spiky-shell toe reshaper is a favourite, and we have the solid fish body wrap.'

'What does that involve?' Tiga asked.

'We insert your body into the mouth of a fish,' the woman said flatly.

'WHY?' Peggy cried.

'To make you beautiful, of course,' said the woman.

Tiga tried not to laugh. 'Actually, we landed here almost completely by accident. We won't be staying.'

'No?' Fran said. 'I quite like the sound of being inserted into a fish and emerging beautiful. Well, *more* beautiful.'

Tiga shook her head. 'No time, Fran. We have to win Witch Wars, remember?' She looked around. 'We just need the exit.'

'You'll need to take a pipe,' the woman said.

Tiga stopped and stared at the woman. She didn't want another trip in a pipe.

The woman pushed open the glass door to reveal a glass platform. Tiga gasped as she peered over the edge.

'Frogcrumpets!' Peggy said.

Fran didn't say anything. She was busy sneakily slipping her foot into a fish's mouth.

Below there were hundreds of glass platforms that went down and down, further than Tiga could see. Long glass walkways connected them. On each platform sat cafés and shops, just like in Ritzy City. Another one had a swimming pool and around the edges were

little glass balconies that looked like they belonged to apartments.

The whole thing was encased in a huge glass dome and hundreds of pipes rained water down on it.

'Is this your first time to Wavely Way?' the woman asked, spotting Tiga and Peggy's mesmerised faces.

They nodded.

'OK, so to leave and get back on land, you take the lift to the very bottom of Wavely Way. Down there is a small door that will shoot you back up to the Docks.'

Tiga looked down. 'Can't we just leave the way we came in?'

'No,' snapped the witch. 'That's the way *in*. Down there is the way *out.*'

She turned, snatched the fish from Fran and stormed off.

'Where do you think the lift is?' Peggy mumbled.

Tiga looked around, but something distracted her. A tiny piece of paper was swirling about in the water outside. It dived to the left and swooped to the right, and Tiga raced down the corridor, her eyes fixed on it.

'What are you doing?' Peggy called after her.

Tiga pointed at the tiny scrap of paper that was now stuck to the glass.

> *wrong way round,*
> *never lose track*
> *I'm bound?*

She inched closer to it and smacked her face on the glass.

'A clue ...' she said.

'Is it?' said Peggy, sounding sceptical.

'It's in that swirly Witch Wars writing, look! *And* it's in the water below the Coves – it's likely that if Felicity Bat was going to destroy the clue she would either take it with her or rip it up there and then and throw it away ...'

'I suppose –' Peggy began, but she was interrupted by someone shouting.

'The disgusting smoke smell is almost completely gone from your hair now!'

'Thank you,' replied someone who sounded very familiar.

Tiga and Peggy looked at each other.

'FLUFFANORA!' they cried before racing down the corridor to the room where their friend was being pampered and prodded and pruned by eight Sunken Ship Road Spa witches.

Tiga burst out laughing when she saw her. Not because a witch was rubbing a fish in her hair but because she was still wearing the jeans! She'd teamed them with a ruffled black top and hundreds of beaded

necklaces that covered her whole neck.

'I couldn't help myself,' said Fluffanora as she pointed at the jeans and smiled.

'*I thought you said you were leaving*,' said the irritable spa witch. She grabbed Tiga's arm.

'Release my friend!' said Fluffanora.

'It's OK,' said Tiga. 'We'd better get going anyway. We sank down here by accident and we need to get back up there. So we have to get the lift to the bottom of Wavely Way and then swim out the exit door back to the top and then –'

'*WHAT?*' said Fluffanora, glaring at the spa witch.

The spa witch looked sheepishly at her feet and backed out of the door.

'Nonsense talk,' said Fluffanora. 'We'll take the hairdryer back to land.'

She patted the seats on either side of her. Above them hung large dome-shaped hairdryers.

Fran coughed.

Fluffanora picked up a small hand-held hairdryer and Fran scuttled over and stood under it.

'Right, now pull the dryer down over your heads,' she said.

And, just like that, the hairdryers started up and they were sucked up and away to somewhere else.

# Ratty Ann

In less than a second they were smack bang back in the middle of Brew's. Hundreds of little witches were stocking the shelves again.

Tiga and Peggy looked at each other. Their hair was now in ridiculously elaborate up-dos.

Fran's hair was also in an elaborate up-do. But, then again, it always was.

'Oh! I almost forgot,' said Tiga, handing Fluffanora the little leather folder of Eddy Eggby's fashion findings.

'For me?' said Fluffanora, beaming at Tiga. She flicked through it.

'The ruffled skirts!'

'I know!' said Tiga.

'The bonnets!'

'I know!' said Tiga.

'Do you still wear those?' Fluffanora asked, sounding a bit disgusted.

'Nah,' said Tiga, 'everything in there is from hundreds of years ago. That's when Eddy Eggby explored above the pipes.'

'This is honestly the best thing anyone has ever given me!' Fluffanora said, squeezing Tiga. 'Thank you so much!'

One of the little Brew's witches poked her head through the clothes hanging on the rail next to them. 'So what's your next move?'

'Yes,' said Fluffanora. 'What now?'

'Felicity Bat stole a clue so we're not really sure …' Tiga explained.

'Oh, I was so annoyed Felicity Bat destroyed a clue before everyone had seen it!' said the little witch, pushing the rail to the side and sending it flying across the room. 'There was talk of getting her disqualified! But it's allowed apparently. I'd call it cheating, but she's playing

 193

it sneaky, just like her gran Celia Crayfish did … At least Crispy found her and is filming her now.'

Tiga's eyes lit up.

'TV, TV, TV, TV, TV, TV, TV!' she cried.

A huge image appeared on the wall of Brew's. It was Felicity Bat and Aggie Hoof. They were walking along a foggy street lined with big black houses and snow-tipped trees.

'Pearl Peak,' said Peggy, stepping so close to the screen she banged into the wall.

'Where's Aggie Hoof's hat?' asked Fran, her nose scrunched and her arms crossed. 'She should have her hat on.'

'The clue must've led them to Pearl Peak. Maybe we should go there,' said Tiga.

'Pearl Peak is miles away. That's a silly move,' said Fluffanora, adjusting Peggy's skew-whiff hat.

Peggy nodded. 'We have to go, though. We have nothing else to go on.'

Fluffanora grabbed a long sequinned jacket from one of the rails.

'*MUUUUUUUUUUUUUUUUUUM!* GET HERE RIGHT NOW! WE NEED A LIFT!'

Fluffanora spotted Tiga and Peggy's shocked faces.

'What?' said Fluffanora. 'We were planning to go for dinner at the Little Leaf restaurant in the treetops a couple of miles from Pearl Peak. And she *loves* driving Ratty Ann.'

'Ratty Ann?' Tiga and Peggy said at the same time.

'Ratty Ann,' Fluffanora said with a smile.

☆⟡☆

Ratty Ann was Mrs Brew's car, but it wasn't like any car Tiga had ever seen before. For starters, it didn't have any sides, just five black squishy sofa-like chairs that were joined together by some sparkly black metal. Each chair had a little table in front of it, apart from one, which had a huge ornate steering wheel. And on each table were grey squares that looked like buttons.

'Oooh, I've heard about these!' Peggy cried as they zoomed along Ritzy City's main street.

Fluffanora turned round. Mrs Brew's head bobbed

along in front, topped with an enormous grey hat with little pompoms round the edge. 'Get some food if you want – you must be starving,' she said.

Tiga was STARVING. Clearly so was Peggy, because she started dribbling.

'Do you know how it works?' Fluffanora called back.

'I think so!' Peggy said, turning to Tiga. 'OK, so this is cool. Each square is a button for the shops and restaurants we're passing. So just say you wanted some shoes from *that* shoe shop there …'

Tiga looked where Peggy was pointing. It was a

shoe shop called Heks's Heels. 'Like Miss Heks!' Tiga laughed.

'Oh yeah!' Peggy laughed. 'Well, you press the Heks's Heels button on your table, and then look! It shows you all the shoes in the shop, and as long as you're not too far away from the shop you just press the ones you want and then it should …' Peggy stared at the table. Tiga heard a noise behind her. She looked round and saw a pair of shoes whizzing through the air. They landed with a little thud on Peggy's table. Peggy pressed a button with a cross on them and then they whizzed away.

'Cool, huh? And so you can do the same with the restaurants you pass. Any restaurants on the grey squares that appear on the table.'

Tiga couldn't believe it. She looked down and scanned the little grey squares. Inventive Ice Creams, Knobbly Noodles, the Gull and Chip Tavern … 'It's AMAZING!' she cried.

Fluffanora shook her head. 'Oh no, not the food at the Gull and Chip Tavern. It's anything but amazing,' she said.

Peggy laughed as a huge bowl of noodles from Knobbly Noodles landed on her table. They weren't like noodles Tiga had seen before – they were all knobbly. She laughed and ordered exactly the same.

'So how is it all going?' Mrs Brew asked. 'I haven't had time to watch *Witch Wars*.'

Fran butted in and explained that Peggy and Tiga had been doing really well, but were now doing really badly. There was the Wavely Way detour and also, Fran explained through gritted teeth, the Brollywood disaster.

'We needed to find out who nominated Tiga for Witch Wars,' Peggy explained.

'And did you?' Mrs Brew asked.

'No,' Tiga said glumly. 'All I know is that they sent this anonymous letter.'

She pulled the letter out of her pocket and a gust of wind nearly whipped it away into the darkness.

'Guard that letter with your life – it's the only evidence you have!' said Fluffanora as Tiga stuffed it back in her pocket.

'An anonymous letter … intriguing,' said Mrs Brew as the car veered on to a dark country road.

'And weird,' Peggy mumbled through a mouthful of noodles. She pressed a button and a huge tower of ice-cream balls landed in front of her. 'Tiga has never met anyone from Sinkville.'

'Well, someone here *must* know you,' said Mrs Brew.

'If she wins, she'll have all the time in the world to look for whoever sent that letter,' Peggy spluttered as she shovelled mouthfuls of ice cream into her mouth. 'But if she loses she'll have to go back to horrible Miss Heks above the pipes.'

Mrs Brew turned round and looked at Tiga.

'You can do it,' she said.

'You'd better do it,' said Fluffanora. 'Ritzy City is so much more fun with you in it. And you brought jeans!'

Peggy nodded enthusiastically – so much so that the ice cream dribbling down her face splattered all over Tiga.

# Camping

Fluffanora and Mrs Brew waved as they sped off into the distance, leaving Tiga and Peggy next to a twisting black road. Up and up the hill it went, before swirling around a tall and pointy white-tipped mountain half hidden in the thick fog.

'Pearl Peak,' Peggy said, pointing at it and yawning. 'You know, it must be really late now. Maybe we should get some sleep and head up there first thing in the morning. I doubt Felicity Bat and Aggie Hoof are doing much at this hour either.'

Tiga mumbled 'TV' a lot and a screen appeared on the road. The coverage of Felicity Bat and Aggie Hoof was just a black screen. It was the same when it clipped to Lizzie Beast and Patty Pigeon.

'See,' Peggy said. 'Everyone has to sleep at some point.'

The screen changed to show them standing at the side of the road.

Peggy waved into Fran's camera.

'Stop that!' Fran said. 'You're not meant to look into the camera! That's rule number one of acting!'

'But we're not acting!' Tiga said. She leapt into view and stuck her tongue out. Peggy started doing a silly dance.

Fran huffed and puffed. 'Ladies, this is not professional.'

Tiga looked around her. On one side of the road was a steep drop and on the other were beautiful leafy trees with spindly branches that dipped down low. The trees were covered in pretty white lights.

'Where do we sleep?' Tiga asked.

Peggy glanced around her. 'Let's camp over here!' she said, taking a couple of steps into the trees. She took off her shoe, just one, and mumbled a spell. 'Little laces and heels in a heap, Make me a better place to sleep.'

'What on EARTH are you doing?' Tiga asked as the shoe began to shake.

'Ah, clever,' said Fran, pointing her camera at the shoe.

The shoe rose up into the air.

*CRACK!*

Peggy moved Tiga backwards slightly as a giant shoe landed with a thud in front of them. There was a small door in the heel.

'Climb in! Climb in!' Peggy said.

When Tiga stepped inside, her eyes grew so wide they looked more like oranges. It wasn't just a big, empty shoe, as she assumed it would be. There was a rickety old kitchen and a wooden table, and some paintings hanging wonkily on the walls. And there was a small, skew staircase that led to two little beds on a wooden balcony overlooking the kitchen.

'This'll do,' Peggy said, straightening up one of the pictures. 'Sorry I don't have better shoes. The better your shoes, the better the place you get.'

Tiga looked down at the shoes Mrs Brew had given her.

'We could try mine …'

'This was a good idea,' said Peggy, fluffing up the pillows on her gigantic bed. Huge pearly chandeliers hung overhead in the sitting room where Tiga was standing. Soft stripy cushions were scattered every-where and there was a swing attached to the ceiling.

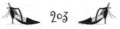

'This reminds me of an old rhyme I heard once,' Tiga said. 'It was about an old woman who lived in a shoe! It said, "She had so many children she didn't know what to do."'

Peggy nodded. 'Yup, she was a witch.'

'What?' Tiga said, jumping on the bed.

'She was a witch,' Peggy repeated. 'She was the one who invented the shoe thing. It changed camping forever. We used to camp in these things called *tents.*'

Tiga laughed. 'We still do that above the pipes.'

'Well, once we win Witch Wars you'll be camping in shoes forever more!' Peggy said, curling up in bed. 'And, just think, you'll be able to make the rules and help other witches ... You could make mean witches wear silly hats when they're nasty. Or you could clean up the horrible parts of Sinkville and make it nicer for the witches who live there, and you could ...'

There was a long silence.

'I could what?' Tiga asked, but Peggy had fallen asleep.

# The Wake-up Call

The swing in the sitting room moved only slightly at first. It creaked forward, and then it creaked back. The pearly chandelier rocked too, and the beds Tiga and Peggy were sleeping in began to shake.

Tiga woke first and shook Peggy.

'Huh, what? Where? Why? Frogs in hats!' Peggy said with a sleepy snort.

There was a bang, and then another one. And another after that.

'Someone's outside,' Tiga whispered.

Peggy leapt to her feet and put on her hat. 'Come on, Tiga.'

They crept to the door. It was shaking.

*Boom.*

Someone was trying to knock it down!

*BOOM.*

Tiga leaned against the door. 'We can't go out there.'

Peggy was peeking out of the kitchen window. 'I can't see anything. The heel is in the way!' She closed the curtains.

The door stopped shaking.

'You try,' a voice outside said.

Tiga looked at Peggy, her eyes wide, and then …

*Knock, knock, knock.*

It was the quietest little knock Tiga had heard. Like a little bird gently tapping the door with a pen.

Tiga took a deep breath and turned the handle.

There, standing in the doorway, light flooding in from behind her, was a familiar little figure.

'Patty Pigeon!' Peggy growled, charging towards her.

'I come in peace! I come in peace!' said Patty, holding her hands in the air.

Sally the fairy hovered in the air next to her and waved. She was hit in the face by a wing belonging to Julie Jumbo Wings.

206

'I'm here too,' Lizzie Beast grunted as she peeked her huge head round the door.

'I think the competition is over,' Patty Pigeon said. 'Can we come in?'

'Over?' Peggy shouted. 'OVER? Ah, frograts, I knew I shouldn't have gone to bed!'

'Well, it's not completely over,' Patty Pigeon explained. 'Felicity Bat and Aggie Hoof are definitely ahead now. We got to the Coves before them – Lizzie swam and I sat on her back – and we saw the clue before they destroyed it, but we can't figure it out. We thought perhaps you could. We don't care about winning; we just definitely don't want Felicity Bat or Aggie Hoof to win. We watched the footage of you that Fran's been filming.'

'It's excellent, isn't it?' said Fran.

Patty Pigeon nodded. 'We think you might have what it takes to beat them and so we want to give you the clue.'

Tiga held her hand to her mouth. 'You want to give me the clue from the Coves?'

207

Lizzie Beast nodded and then pointed at Patty Pigeon, who recited perfectly:

> *'I see most things in circles,*
> *At times the wrong way round,*
> *But why is it I never lose track*
> *Of where it is I'm bound?'*

Peggy laughed. It sounded a lot like a relieved laugh. But Tiga eyed the other witches suspiciously.

'How do we know this isn't a trap? You could've just made that clue up. You could be working with Felicity Bat.'

Patty Pigeon took a step forward, her hands clasped neatly in front of her. 'I can assure you that is not the case: Felicity Bat and I are NOT friends. Peggy, you know that.'

'It's true,' said Peggy. 'Felicity Bat is always lifting her up by the pigtails and levitating up *really* high and then dropping her on prickly hedges.'

Patty Pigeon shivered. 'And into swamps, and down

small holes, and once down a chimney, and on to a lamp post, and into many bins, and once through the roof of Cakes, Pies and That's About It Really.'

Tiga nodded at Peggy and put her arm round Patty. 'OK, let's figure out this clue. What moves in circles and at times the wrong way round?'

'How can you move in a circle the wrong way round? Peggy asked. 'It's a *circle*.'

'And it never loses track …' Tiga mumbled.

'Track, like train tracks perhaps,' suggested Peggy.

Tiga leapt about on the spot and hugged her. 'Sort of like a train, only it goes backwards and it circles! The answer is a ROLLER COASTER! Didn't Aggie Hoof say Sinkville's only roller coaster is in Pearl Peak?'

'YES!' Peggy and Patty Pigeon cried.

'WOOHOO!' Lizzie Beast cheered, jumping up and knocking one of the chandeliers off the ceiling. It fell to the ground and smashed.

And squashed Patty Pigeon.

'Ouch!' she cried from under it. Then Tiga saw the smoke.

Lizzie Beast gasped. 'I didn't mean to –'

She lifted the pearly chandelier off Patty Pigeon. Smoke was billowing up her legs.

Fran wiggled in the air. 'Wait for the pop!'

Tiga, Peggy and Lizzie Beast glared at her as Patty Pigeon disappeared with a pop.

'What?' said Fran. 'I love the pop.'

# PATTY PIGEON IS OUT!

The girl for whom nobody in Sinkville has been cheering is out!

**Reporter:** Patty, most of us forgot you were in the competition because Lizzie Beast has been blocking the camera, and now she's accidentally knocked you out. Are you angry? Are you FURIOUS?

**Patty Pigeon:** Um, I don't *think* so ...

**Reporter:** WILL YOU BE GETTING REVENGE ON LIZZIE BEAST FOR RUINING YOUR CHANCES OF WINNING?

**Patty Pigeon:** Pardon?

**Reporter:** WILL YOU BE KEEPING A BEADY EYE ON HER, WATCHING HER EVERY MOVE, WAITING FOR THE CHANCE TO GET YOUR REVENGE?'

**Patty Pigeon:** You're scaring me ...

NOTE FROM THE *RITZY CITY POST* EDITOR: THIS INTERVIEW ENDED BECAUSE OUR REPORTER TERRIFIED PATTY PIGEON.

And so a final word from Patty Pigeon's fairy, Sally.

**Reporter:** Sally ... Sally? Where's Sally? Did someone check Sally wasn't squashed under the chandelier?

# Battle at
# Pearl Peak

'And that's the smallest house in Pearl Peak,' Peggy said, pointing at a huge house that had so many floors it looked like some sort of elaborate stone wedding cake. 'And that shop, Beyond Bling, sells the most expensive jewellery in Sinkville, and that restaurant, Silly Expensive, has the most expensive food in Sinkville. And that's a money tree, and that's …'

Tiga had never seen anything like it. Pearl Peak was dark, cold and enveloped in fog, but the buildings were slick and shiny – almost clinical. All the trees were exactly the same shape, as if they weren't really real. And in the distance stood a perfect snow-covered castle, with a big black roller coaster wrapped around it.

It was eerily quiet. Not a single witch stood on the icy street.

Well, not at first …

'Welcome to Pearl Peak,' Felicity Bat said as she glided towards them through the fog.

'Thank yo–' Peggy began, but then realised it was Felicity Bat and Felicity was not being nice.

'I'm sorry you made it this far. I'm going to have to knock off your heads now,' she sneered.

Aggie Hoof cackled and tugged at Felicity Bat's arm. 'Let's get rid of the annoying one from above the pipes first.'

Felicity Bat set her eyes on Tiga and snaked towards her. 'There's something you need to know, Pipe Witch. You aren't welcome here. Not in Pearl Peak, not anywhere in Sinkville. Witches like you don't deserve to be here. It's time you went back to your horrible little life up there.' She rose up into the air, but not – for once – because she was levitating. It was because Lizzie Beast had lifted her up by the belt of her dress. She took off Felicity Bat's hat and handed it to Tiga.

Felicity Bat waved her hand and Lizzie Beast started to float.

'She's making Lizzie Beast levitate!' Peggy said, stomping her feet. 'Squash her shrivelled head, Tiga!'

Tiga pulled the shrivelled head off the hat and dropped it on the ground.

*It can't be this easy?!* she thought. *Felicity Bat has won GAS awards …*

With a shaky foot raised in the air, she looked up at Felicity Bat and smiled.

But then Felicity Bat did something odd.

She smiled back.

Tiga crunched the shrivelled head under her shoe and waited for the smoke to billow up Felicity Bat's legs.

They all waited.

Peggy waited.

Lizzie Beast floated about in the air, and waited.

Felicity Bat waited.

And then …

'Aaaaah!' came a cry.

Tiga spun round. There, behind Peggy, arms outstretched, about to attack, stood Aggie Hoof with smoke billowing from her shoes.

'She was wearing Aggie Hoof's hat!' Peggy shouted.

'You mean cheat!' Tiga cried.

'YOU CRUSHED MY SHRIVELLED HEAD!' Aggie Hoof roared, before disappearing with a pop.

'THE POP!' Fran cheered.

Tiga spun round again just in time to hear another crunch.

'OH NO!' Peggy cried, racing over to Lizzie Beast.

She was lying in a heap on the floor, smoke surrounding her. Julie Jumbo Wings was flapping about in her face trying to help her, but she was only slapping her with her wings.

'Ouch. Wings. Ouch. Wings. Ouch. Wings,' Lizzie Beast said.

Tiga raced towards Felicity Bat, who was levitating high up in the air and cackling like a mad witch.

'Where is your hat, Felicity Bat?' Tiga demanded.

'Wouldn't you like to know,' she said before tearing through the sky, leaving only the echo of her cackles behind. Oh, and Crispy, who was lolling about in the air looking droopy and bored.

Fran gave Crispy a stern look.

'Oh, right, better follow her,' said the fairy as she adjusted the camera and flew off.

'LET'S GET HER!' Peggy roared as Lizzie Beast disappeared with a wave and a pop.

Tiga paused.

They *could* race after Felicity Bat, try to find her hat and knock off her shrivelled head – it was probably still

on the bed at Linden House – but they still needed to figure out the last clue. Maybe Felicity Bat hadn't worked it out yet! When Tiga said that to Peggy, Peggy hid her hand behind her back.

'What is it?' Tiga asked.

'Um,' Peggy said, showing Tiga the TV on her hand. *FELICITY BAT FINDS FINAL CLUE AND RACES TO THE FINISH*, said the words running along the bottom of the screen.

'Frogankles,' Tiga grumbled. 'Big frogankles.'

# AGGIE HOOF AND LIZZIE BEAST ARE OUT!

Pearl Peak's richest kid and Ritzy City's most gigantic girl are the latest to be knocked out of Witch Wars! Our reporter caught up with them to find out what it feels like to be so close, and yet so frogging far.

**Reporter:** Aggie Hoof, Lizzie Beast, talk to me.

**Aggie Hoof:** I WILL ONLY SPEAK TO *TOAD* MAGAZINE AND I WILL NOT BE INTERVIEWED WITH *HER*.

**Reporter:** I'm afraid you were knocked out at almost exactly the same time so you and Lizzie Beast have to be in the same article. Now, tell me –

**Aggie Hoof:** NO!

**Reporter:** Your best friend Felicity Bat is the reason you were knocked out. She was wearing your hat and didn't seem to care when you were knocked out.

219

**Aggie Hoof:** SHE CARES.
**Reporter:** Have you watched the footage of Witch Wars since you left? She really doesn't seem to care.
**Aggie Hoof:** I AM TERMINATING THIS INTERVIEW.

NOTE FROM THE *RITZY CITY POST* EDITOR: AGGIE HOOF TERMINATED THE INTERVIEW AND OUR REPORTER FORGOT TO INTERVIEW LIZZIE BEAST, SO THIS IS IT. AGGIE HOOF REFUSED TO LET US TAKE HER PICTURE, SO HERE IS A PICTURE OF LIZZIE BEAST, AND A PICTURE OF LIZZIE BEAST DRESSED AS AGGIE HOOF.

And now, some final words from Lizzie Beast's fairy, Julie Jumbo Wings, and Aggie Hoof's fairy, Donna.

**Donna:** What do you think of my hair?

**Julie Jumbo Wings:** It's just JULIE!

# Peggy Screaming on a Roller Coaster

The two witches climbed on the roller coaster and as Peggy pulled down the black bar on the seat it burst into life. Lights flashed, chirpy music started up and a voice bellowed, 'WELCOME TO THE HAIR-MESSING, MIND-BENDING, WITCHINGLY WILD ROLLER COASTER RIDE OF YOUR LIFE!'

Below them stood a large crowd of witches in the blackest of black dresses. They didn't cheer or whoop or whistle for Tiga and Peggy, but remained deadly silent. It was clear whose side they were on.

The roller coaster shot forward and spun round in loops.

'We don't have time for this!' Tiga cried.

'MAYBE THE CLUE WILL BE HANGING FROM THE ROLLER COASTER SOMEWHERE AND WE'LL NEED TO GRAB IT!' Peggy screamed in Tiga's ear.

Tiga sighed. She had almost given up and was feeling sick, but as the roller coaster did a triple loop and swirled around and dived back down, some swirly writing appeared in front of them.

> *The end can be found where the start once sat.*
> *Touch the Giant Pin, and that will be that.*
> *You'll find it in daylight, at dawn and at night,*
> *Just not on a Wednesday, no matter your might.*

'DID YOU SEE THAT?!' Peggy roared in Tiga's ear as the roller coaster screeched to a halt.

Tiga steadied herself as she stepped out of the carriage. 'Well, the end can be found where the start once sat. We started at Linden House, so it must mean there.'

'It might mean at the top of Pearl Peak. That's where the first witch landed. Maybe it means the start of Sinkville, not Witch Wars,' Peggy said.

224

Tiga paced back and forth. 'It could mean that …'

'What's the Giant Pin bit about?' Peggy asked. 'I've never heard of a Giant Pin, and it's not a place.'

Tiga continued to pace back and forth in front of Peggy as Peggy flicked through the useless history of Sinkville book.

'We could just do the TV spell and see where Felicity Bat has gone!' Peggy suggested.

'But she might be wrong,' said Tiga. 'We have the clue, we have all we need to solve it. We can do it.'

Peggy threw the history of Sinkville book on the floor. 'There is nothing in here about a Giant Pin.'

*What does it mean?* Tiga thought. She started to pace faster and faster. *Think, Tiga Whicabim, think, you big witch!*

'You've stopped,' said Peggy.

Tiga was frozen on the spot. A huge grin spread like jam across her face.

'It's an anagram! Like my name! When you mix up the letters of Tiga Whicabim it spells *I am a big witch*.'

Peggy snorted. 'That's brilliant.'

 225

'And,' Tiga said, her grin getting unfathomably big, 'what word do you get if you jumble up the letters in Giant Pin?'

Peggy scrunched up her face and thought for a moment. 'You get … PAINTING!'

'We have to find a painting!' Tiga cried.

'Amazing!' Peggy said, leaping from foot to foot. 'Which painting?'

Tiga's mouth opened, and then shut again. 'I'm not entirely sure … It must be in Linden House – that's where we started, like the first bit of the clue says. And Fran did say Linden House is home to all of Sinkville's most important artworks. It must be a painting in Linden House.'

'I did say that! I say many great things,' said Fran.

'What do you think the day and dawn and night but not Wednesday means?' Peggy asked.

Tiga's eyes widened. 'The hidden painting of the map of Sinkville! The one you get to via the spinning sofa! That room doesn't exist on a Wednesday! Does it, Fran? … Fran?'

Fran had vanished.

'YES!' Peggy cried. 'THAT'S IT!'

'Where is Fran?' Tiga asked. 'She was here just a moment ago …'

'No time for Fran,' said Peggy. 'If Felicity Bat is already on her way there, we're never going to beat her. Linden House is miles and miles from Pearl Peak.'

'There must be a quicker way,' Tiga mumbled. And then she remembered something. 'Pegs, do you know where the Pearl Peak bookshop is?'

Peggy looked confused. 'Now, Tiga, I *love* books, but this is no time for book shopping.'

Tiga grabbed her arm. 'There's a shortcut to the Towers in the Pearl Peak bookshop. I saw it on one of the towers when we were there. And the Towers is much closer to Linden House than Pearl Peak.'

Peggy squealed and they raced down the hill to a little bookshop. The outside was covered in frost and the inside was stuffed with black books.

'No, of course you can't take the shortcut,' a grumpy witch with small round glasses said.

227

'MOTHER, MY DOLL IS MISSING!' a little witch next to her squealed. 'MY DOLL IS MISSING! MISSING!'

'You know,' said Peggy, 'you should look in a little doll shop in the Docks called Desperate Dolls. The witch who owns the shop collects all the lost dolls in Sinkville and, er, fixes them.'

This seemed to please the little witch. 'She's good. Let her use the shortcut, Mother. LET HER USE THE SHORTCUT, MOTHER!'

The grumpy witch growled and rolled her eyes. 'Oh, *fine*. Use the shortcut.'

Peggy and Tiga tore towards the hole in the ground and jumped.

# Felicity Bat Soars
# into the Lead

B ack in Ritzy City, Felicity Bat strolled along the road
with a smirk on her face. She had so much time on
her hands that she didn't even have to levitate any more.

A roar sounded around her.

'Peggy and Tiga figured out the clue!' an old witch
yelled.

'One of them might still win it!' another cried.

'Shhh, guys, that's Felicity Bat over there,' another
whispered.

Felicity Bat growled and flew fast towards Linden
House.

# Thanks, Karen

As Tiga pelted down the street towards Linden House, she could see a huge crowd gathered outside. Only three flags remained.

'There are thousands of witches!' Peggy cried. 'What are they looking at?'

Tiga stopped suddenly.

Peggy flew into the back of her and knocked her hat off. Tiga dived and caught it just before it hit the ground.

'Sorry!' Peggy shouted, leaping from foot to foot.

They were both panicking, and Tiga knew that wasn't good.

She held up her hand and mumbled the TV spell. Felicity Bat was in Linden House. She was taking all the

paintings off the walls and lining them up in the bare sitting room with the flowery sofa. The room that would lead her to the map!

'She doesn't know which painting it is!' Tiga cried. 'She doesn't know about the sofa and the map – she arrived too late, remember? She wasn't with us when we looked at the map, and she wasn't one of the girls in the room when we flipped back round on the sofa. All she knows is that the answer to the clue is a painting in Linden House!'

'We could still beat her,' Peggy said.

Tiga lowered her voice to a whisper. 'And without Fran no one will be filming us, so Felicity Bat won't be able to tell where we are. We can sneak in … Do you think Fran is OK?'

'I'm sure she's fine …' said Peggy, not sounding very sure at all. 'Or at least probably not dead.'

'It *is* Fran,' said Tiga. 'She's indestructible.'

'You're right,' Peggy said. 'She's definitely not squashed somewhere. And she would want us to carry on …'

Tiga nodded. She held up her hand and showed Peggy the image of Felicity Bat in Linden House. She wasn't wearing her hat.

'Pegs, we need to be clever about this. She doesn't have her hat and she's in the very room we need to get to. I say we try to find her hat and crush her shrivelled head. If we can't find it, we create a distraction and get her out of there so we can get to the map.'

Peggy nodded. 'Let's just hope she doesn't sit on that sofa …'

☆⭐☆

Tiga and Peggy sneaked round the back of Linden House to avoid the crowd that was getting bigger and bulkier by the second.

They found an open window by the kitchen and raced upstairs to Felicity Bat's room. There, placed carefully on the bed, was the hat they needed.

Tiga grabbed it, her hands shaking, and felt for the shrivelled head.

'The shrivelled head isn't here,' she whispered.

Peggy grabbed the hat and felt around the brim. 'Where could it be?'

'MORE WITCH WARS WITCHES!' a voice suddenly cried. It belonged to the witch with the ladder; she was peering in through the window again.

Peggy dropped the hat. Tiga froze. And that's when they heard the sound of angry footsteps clattering up the stairs.

'Hide!' Peggy shouted.

'Run!' Tiga cried, grabbing Peggy's arm and charging out into the hallway.

They crashed straight into Felicity Bat.

'Well, well, well. You thought you could sneak in and beat me, did you? You of all people, Piggy, should know I'm much too clever for you. You're rubbish at everything. You're a waste of Sinkville space. You should just go and live with your little friend above the pipes. Everyone would be glad to see you go. No one wants you here, Piggy.'

'Ooooooooh,' went the crowd outside.

'Oh, I've had enough of your nastiness!' Tiga said.

'What have you done with your shrivelled head, you horrible witch?'

Felicity Bat found this hilarious. 'You know being a bad witch is actually considered a good thing down here.'

Crispy nodded as she buzzed around Felicity Bat's head.

'NO, IT'S NOT!' the woman on the ladder yelled.

Felicity Bat flicked her finger and sent her flying.

There was a crunching sound, and then a gasp, and then a very faint, 'I'm OK …'

Felicity Bat cleared her throat and continued. 'I'm incredibly good at everything I do, and you'll never figure out where I've hidden my shrivelled head. It's somewhere you'll never find it.'

'The half empty cereal box on the dining room table,' said Karen. She was standing in the window, perched on the ladder. She winked at Tiga.

'*KAAAAREHHHN, YOU IDIOOOOOOT!*' came a cry from outside. Aggie Hoof was obviously watching from the crowd.

Felicity Bat stared at Tiga.

Tiga stared at Felicity Bat.

Then Tiga made a run for it. She shot down the stairs, but her legs wouldn't move fast enough! Felicity Bat was tearing through the air behind her.

'Aaaaaargh, you won't get it!' she screeched.

They were getting closer and closer to the dining room. Felicity Bat flung her hands madly about in the air, sending statues crashing down on Tiga. Tiga ducked and dived and threw herself towards the dining room door, but before she could reach it, it slammed shut.

She crashed into it and fell to the floor as Felicity Bat cackled.

Everything seemed to move in slow motion for Tiga. She groaned, clutching her head. There was no hat on it any more. She looked up slowly and saw Felicity Bat hovering above her. In her hand was Tiga's hat, and on it was the only thing keeping her in Ritzy City.

'You know, when I crush this they'll send you straight back up the pipes. You won't be interviewed by the rubbish *Ritzy City Post* reporter and you won't get to see

who wins, although I think we all know it's going to be me. You'll be back above the pipes, all alone with that horrible woman you hate. And no one in Ritzy City will ever remember you were here.'

Tiga clenched her fists and tried not to cry. She bit her lip and glanced up the stairs. Peggy was nowhere to be seen. All she wanted was to say goodbye to Peggy.

'I suppose it's terribly unoriginal,' Felicity Bat said. 'But ... any last words?'

The door to the dining room flew open.

'YES! IT'S PEGGY, *NOT* PIGGY!!'

Peggy held up a shrivelled head and smashed it on the ground.

Felicity Bat's mouth fell open. 'What? How did you –? You were upstairs!'

'The nice but nosey witch let me borrow her ladder and I climbed down and sneaked back in through the dining room window. I'm not *that* stupid,' Peggy said with a smile.

Smoke swirled around Felicity Bat's legs.

'Wha–? I don't ... This wasn't meant TO HAPPEN!'

 237

She bellowed the words as she spun into the dining room, clutching Tiga's shrivelled head.

Tiga and Peggy raced after her.

Felicity Bat screamed and hurled the head across the room. Tiga gasped, but it floated gently back into her hand.

'She's out,' Peggy said with a smile. 'So she can't destroy your shrivelled head any more.'

'Aaaaaaargh!' Felicity Bat roared as black smoke engulfed her.

Tiga hugged Peggy so tightly that Peggy's voice was more of a squeak when she said, 'We should go to the map.'

They walked arm in arm to the little flowery sofa. Tiga looked back and smiled just as Felicity Bat disappeared.

With a pop.

# FELICITY BAT IS OUT!

The relative of Ritzy City's most evil ruling witches – and the witch deemed most likely to win Witch Wars – is *finally* out! Our reporter tracked her down at the Gull and Chip Tavern and asked her a few questions.

**Reporter:** Did you think the hat thing was clever? Because it was at first and then it seemed, well, a bit stupid.

**Felicity Bat:** This isn't the end. That girl from above the pipes can't win. She doesn't deserve it.

**Reporter:** So you'd like Peggy Pigwiggle to win?

**Felicity Bat:** Don't be ridiculous!

**Reporter:** Well, it's her or the girl from above the pipes ...

**Felicity Bat:** Well, for now ...

**Reporter:** What does that mean?

NOTE FROM THE *RITZY CITY POST* EDITOR: OUR REPORTER FORGOT TO WRITE DOWN THE LAST PART OF THIS INTERVIEW. SORRY.

And so, a final word from Felicity Bat's fairy, Crispy.

**Crispy:** FREEEEEEEEDOOOOOM!

**Reporter:** You make a lot of noise for such a little thing ...

# The Painting

'Well, it looks like whoever thought I could win Witch Wars was right!' Tiga said, waving the anonymous letter in the air. It slipped out of her fingers and fell to the floor. Peggy picked it up.

'And this must be the answer to the final clue,' Tiga said, prodding the wall with her finger.

'This letter smells funny,' said Peggy, sniffing it.

'We just need to figure out what we have to do with the map …' Tiga mumbled.

'It smells very faintly of rotten socks,' said Peggy.

Without looking away from the map, Tiga grabbed the letter out of Peggy's hand and smelled it. 'It's cheese,' she said. 'Maybe we need to touch the right bit of the painting or something …'

'Cheese?' Peggy asked. 'What's that?'

'You know,' Tiga said. '*Cheese.*'

'I've never heard of it. It must be an above the pipes thing.'

Very slowly, Tiga turned to face Peggy. She had a flashback to her conversation with Fran in the shed.

*What? You're not coming with me to Ritzy City, a place of wonder and absolutely no cheese?*

*… a place of wonder and absolutely no cheese …*

*… absolutely no cheese …*

'Are you OK?' Peggy asked.

In that moment it felt like all of Sinkville had fallen on Tiga's head. Her knees buckled and she collapsed on the floor.

'What's wrong?' Peggy cried.

Tiga held the letter as far away from her as she could and turned it from one side to the other. 'Miss Heks,' she said in amazement. 'It was Miss Heks.'

'What? Miss Heks wrote the letter of nomination?' Peggy asked. 'How do you know?'

Tiga slowly got to her feet. 'The cheese, Peggy, the

cheese … Her cheese water. Of *course*, it makes sense. Miss Heks does look a lot like a witch who has been in the pipes. And the houses in the Docks – remember I said they were just like the one I live in with Miss Heks? Maybe she was one of the witches who left during that Big Exit Fran was talking about. She nominated me!'

Tiga grinned a victorious grin.

'But *why*?' Peggy asked.

Tiga stopped grinning. 'I don't know.'

'Tiga,' Peggy said, suddenly distracted. 'Does Linden House look like it's lit up on the map to you?'

Tiga moved closer to the wall. Sure enough, there was a tiny light coming from Linden House. Tiga touched it and moved her finger slightly. A thin line of light appeared where her finger had been. She dragged her finger to the Towers and it lit up too!

'Maybe we have to trace the route of all the clues!' she said. 'If we trace it together, at exactly the same time, maybe we'll both win!'

Peggy moved her finger across the map too.

'From Linden House,' they said together, 'to the

Towers! Down to Desperate Dolls in the Docks! To the Coves! Then the Underwater World, oh no, we weren't meant to go there, it was then to Pearl Peak! And from Pearl Peak BACK TO LINDEN HOUSE!'

The lines of light glowed on the map.

Nothing happened.

'Was something meant to happen?' Tiga asked just as there was a massive *BANG* and everything went black.

# Winning

'Congratulations,' Julie Jumbo Wings said flatly. 'You've both got to the end now, at the same time, but only one can win, so now you need to fight until one of your shrivelled heads is crushed.'

Tiga and Peggy had landed back on the steps of Linden House. The huge crowd roared and cheered and whooped and one person said 'ROCKETS!' which made no sense, so everyone ignored it.

'Where's Fran?' Tiga asked. 'Isn't this her job?'

'Hurt her wing on the roller coaster,' Julie Jumbo Wings said. 'She's walking back from Pearl Peak. She's almost back, but it's taking a while, what with her little legs and everything.'

Tiga suddenly felt awful. *Poor Fran*, she thought.

*I didn't notice her hurt wing. She seemed fine after the roller coaster …*

'OK, let's do this!' Peggy said, ripping the shrivelled head off the rim of her hat and holding it high in the air. 'You are one shrivelled head away from living in Ritzy City forever! As the RULER OF SINKVILLE!'

The crowd cheered.

'Oh, before I forget!' Peggy said, rummaging in her pocket.

She handed Tiga her notebook.

'Just some ideas,' she said with a smile. 'And some people you should help.'

Tiga stared down at the tattered notebook in her hands. She wiped away a bit of hair gunk that was stuck to the corner and smiled.

Peggy raised her shrivelled head in the air and squeezed her eyes shut. 'One … two …'

'Wait!' Tiga cried, grabbing Peggy's arm. 'Don't smash that yet.'

'What? But I have to.'

Tiga smiled. 'Peggy, you are the kindest person in all

247

of Sinkville.' She took off her hat. 'And that's why you should win Witch Wars.'

The crowd gasped.

'But that makes no sense. You'd have to go back above the pipes and live with horrible Miss Heks!'

'But, Peggy, Sinkville needs you. I have no idea how to run this city. I can't even do any spells. Anyway, I have unfinished business with Miss Heks. I want to know why she nominated me.'

'You're just saying that so I don't feel bad about winning! But I do feel bad! I want to help you,' Peggy said. 'And, anyway, I'm not smart enough to rule Sinkville.'

'You *are*,' Tiga said. 'You solved most of the clues.'

'I didn't –'

'And you taught me some spells.'

'Hardly any.'

'And you beat Felicity Bat, winner of many GAS awards.'

Peggy grinned. 'I did beat Felicity Bat.'

'This place needs you, Peggy. It needs someone good

with lots of brilliant ideas.' She handed the notebook back to Peggy. 'Witch Wars has always been your battle.'

'For a while it looked like it was going to be Felicity Bat's battle!' a witch yelled from the crowd.

'But the old witch said the *elegant* witch would win. That can't be me ...' Peggy mumbled.

Tiga rolled her eyes. 'Oh, what has being elegant got to do with being good at ruling Sinkville? That witch was talking nonsense.'

'GO, PEGGY! YOU CAN DO IT!' shouted someone from the crowd. It was Lily Cranberry from the Coves. She'd obviously left the Coves for the first time in thousands of years to watch the end of *Witch Wars*. And she'd brought hundreds of her fellow party witches with her.

'PE-GGY, PE-GGY, PE-GGY!' they all chanted.

Patty Pigeon and Lizzie Beast joined in. 'PE-GGY! PE-GGY!'

'Pe-ggy, Pe-ggy, Pe-ggy!' shouted the bald witch from the tower, in her big wig.

'PE-GGY! PE-GGY!' shouted the little witch from Pearl Peak bookshop, waving a tattered doll in the air.

Peggy stared at the crowd in amazement.

'See,' said Tiga. 'They want you to win!'

'Pe-ggy, Pe-ggy, Pe-ggy!' shouted Mrs Clutterbuck, clapping her hands.

'PE-GGY, PE-GGY, PE-GGY!'

The shouts got louder, and witches started stomping their feet.

Peggy spun round, taking it all in.

The witch with the ladder waved and shouted, 'PE-GGY!' and Peggy's mum chanted too and wiped away the streams of tears rolling down her face. She was standing next to Mrs Brew and Fluffanora who were smiling sad smiles. A bunch of Brew's witches stood next to her, leaping up and down squealing, 'Pe-ggy, Pe-ggy, Pe-ggy!'

Tiga took a deep breath and dropped her shrivelled head to the ground.

*CRUNCH.*

She could feel cold smoke swirling around her feet almost instantly.

'Peggy, well done. You are Top Witch of Ritzy City and all that lies beyond,' Julie Jumbo Wings said flatly.

'OH, THAT'S NOT HOW IT'S DONE!' Fran scoffed, pushing Julie Jumbo Wings out of the way and shooting glittery dust everywhere (mostly in Peggy's mouth again).

'I thought your wing was broken,' Julie Jumbo Wings said suspiciously.

'Well, I did too, Julie Jumbo Wings, but then it started working again, so there.' She turned to Tiga and winked.

Tiga smiled. But then she stared down at her feet and realised that this was it. She would never see Fran again.

'Can't she stay in Linden House with me?' Peggy asked. 'I'll look after her!'

Fran shook her head. 'Oh no, you're just children! You can't look after each other.'

'But …' Peggy said, 'you're letting me rule all of Ritzy City and beyond.'

Fran spluttered, 'That's *completely* different. It is one thing to trust someone to make laws. It is quite another to trust them to brush their teeth and go to bed on time.'

Tiga nodded as the smoke moved further up her legs. 'That does make sense.'

'DOES IT?' Peggy wailed.

'And Miss Heks is Tiga's guardian,' Fran said. 'We can't just steal her away now, can we?'

Tiga knew Fran was right, although she wished she wasn't.

Fran turned to Tiga. 'Tiga, I'm so sorry. There is nothing I can do.'

Tiga nodded. She glanced around at the place in all its black, grey and white glory. She wished she didn't have to leave. The smoke was now all the way up to her neck.

'I'll find a way of getting you back!' Peggy cried as Tiga's vision began to blur.

And then, with an annoying little pop, she was gone.

# Home

Tiga slid slowly up the pipe, tears running down her face, along with a lot of sludge and slime. She could feel her hat being smooshed and the beautiful black lace of her dress tearing around her legs.

She emerged in the shed, all tattered and torn and covered in gunk.

Her hat, now pointy, was sitting at a jaunty angle on top of her head. She stood hunched in the shed and exhaled.

She was home.

Well, sort of. The shed looked incredibly different. Instead of the old mouldy wooden walls, they were sleek and painted with multi-coloured stripes, with lots of shelves. Shelves filled with cheese.

Miss Heks threw the door open and stomped in, her arms full of cheese. When she saw Tiga, she froze. The lumps of cheese in her hands fell to the floor.

'Tiga Whicabim,' she seethed.

# PEGGY PIGWIGGLE WINS WITCH WARS!

The clumsy little thing whom everyone thought would be the first one out has won Witch Wars and is now Top Witch of Sinkville! Our reporter sat down with her in her grand new home, Linden House, and asked her some questions ...

**Reporter:** Why do you look so sad? You're rich and powerful now!

**Peggy:** My only friend is gone and I need to figure out how to get her back.

**Reporter:** But you won. Aren't you just a little bit like: 'YES, I WON! I WON! I WOOOOOOOOON!'

**Peggy:** No.

**Reporter:** Ah.

**Peggy:** Anything else?

**Reporter:** Yes! What will be your first rule change?

**Peggy:** No more riding on cleaners. All cleaners once travelled on can ride on their witches for one week.

NOTE FROM THE *RITZY CITY POST* EDITOR: WAIT, I THINK OUR REPORTER JUST DID AN ENTIRE INTERVIEW WITHOUT MESSING IT UP.

And now a final word from Peggy's fairy, Bow.

**Bow:** I'm so glad Peggy won! I like to think I played a big part in her success.

**Reporter:** Bow, we all know you weren't there.

# The Visitors

'I can't believe you didn't win,' Miss Heks bellowed.

'I *knew* it was you!' Tiga said, pointing her finger at the witch.

'You are NEVER to set foot in this shed again! I want you in the kitchen stirring the cheese water. AND THAT IS ALL YOU WILL DO FROM NOW ON.'

Tiga stood tall and took a step forward. 'You're one of the Big Exit witches, aren't you?'

Miss Heks bowed. 'Well, aren't you clever?' she said sarcastically.

'Why did you nominate me?'

'Wanted to get rid of you, let that vile place down there deal with you.'

'It's not a vile place!' Tiga yelled.

If Tiga hadn't been yelling quite so loudly, she would've heard the scratching noise in the sink behind her.

'IT'S THE MOST BEAUTIFUL PLACE, FULL OF THE MOST BEAUTIFUL PEOPLE! And a couple of evil ones. BUT MOSTLY BEAUTIFUL PEOPLE!'

Miss Heks grunted and pointed past Tiga to the sink, where three disgustingly tattered witches and a fairy now stood.

'Peggy?' Tiga said.

'My nose feels funny,' said Peggy, rubbing a slightly flattened nose. Next to her stood what looked like Mrs Brew and Fluffanora. Mrs Brew's hat tapered to a long spindly point and then flopped over at the end. Her dress was in tatters. Fluffanora was ninety per cent slime.

'They weren't lying about pipe travel,' she grumbled.

'What are you doing here?' Tiga cried. She wanted to hug them, but she thought it best to stand squarely in the middle of the room, creating a barrier between her Ritzy City friends and evil Miss Heks.

'We are here to take you back home to Ritzy City,' Fluffanora said as she turned towards Miss Heks. 'We want to adopt Tiga. She belongs with us.'

Miss Heks cackled. '*Adopt.*'

'My mum here, Mrs Brew, said she would,' Fluffanora went on, pushing Mrs Brew forward.

'I would love to,' said Mrs Brew. 'That's if you'd like me to, Tiga?'

'YES!' Tiga screamed, so loudly and so close to Miss Heks's ear that she winced and growled as Tiga ran, arms outstretched, towards her three favourite witches, knocking them clean over.

They all slowly turned to Miss Heks to see her reaction.

The old bat stood frozen to the spot. The stench of cheese combined with the length of time it was taking her to respond made the whole thing excruciating.

Finally, she puffed out her cheeks, put her hands on her hips and yelled, 'TAKE THE BRAT! I'll be glad to be rid of her.'

 260

Tiga stared up at her in disbelief. 'Really?'

'I've been trying to find a way to get rid of her for years,' said Miss Heks. 'Useless thing couldn't even win Witch Wars!'

'She could've won, but she let me win,' Peggy said.

Miss Heks narrowed her eyes at Tiga. 'Weak.'

'Well, if that's everything,' Mrs Brew said, grabbing on to the sink and pulling herself upright again, 'I think we'll be off.'

Tiga scooped up the little slug on the sink and put it in her pocket, and the four of them linked arms.

'Bye, Miss Heks,' she said.

Miss Heks grunted.

And then they were gone.

'IT'S JUST AS BAD GOING IN THIS DIRECTION!' Fluffanora shouted.

'Miss Heks,' came a voice from the rocking chair. 'Have you ever thought of storing something less pungent than cheese in here? Flowers perhaps? Or bicycles?'

'OUT,' Miss Heks said without even looking where the voice was coming from.

'All right, all right,' Fran grumbled as she soared towards the sink. 'Wait for me!'

# Party in Ritzy

All up and down the street in Ritzy City, people were dancing. The sound of music filled the air, and little lanterns bobbed about above the heads of all the happy witches.

'Clutterbucks?' said a witch holding a tray of drinks.

Mrs Brew squeezed Tiga. 'Ritzy City is now exactly how it should be.'

'You're back! FOREVER!' squealed Peggy, skipping on the spot.

Fluffanora dived into the crowd of dancers and started pushing people out of the way to make room for her twirling.

Tiga spotted Felicity Bat standing in the shadows, her arms folded. She glared at Tiga. Aggie Hoof was

next to her, on her hands and knees, and sitting on top of her was Karen, who was grinning madly. She gave Tiga the thumbs up.

'Peggy ... Have you been making up new rules already?' Tiga asked.

Peggy smiled and waved at Karen. Aggie Hoof rolled her eyes.

'Dance!' Mrs Brew said, gently nudging the pair of them towards the crowd.

'Make room for meeeeeee!' screeched Fran as she shot into the middle.

☆⭐☆

Tiga danced for hours that night with the crowds from Ritzy City. They laughed and joked and drank Clutterbucks, and talked for hours about the old witch with the cart of disgusting hats and how her prediction had been so wrong. It wasn't an elegant witch who'd won – it was the dishevelled and brilliant Peggy Pigwiggle.

'First time the old witch has been wrong!' someone said.

'She was SO wrong!' another cried.

'She shouldn't be allowed to wear that "I am never wrong" badge!'

But the old witch just stood behind her cart and watched them. Her wrinkly lips scrunched and spread into a crooked little grin, because she knew everything, and she knew exactly what was coming next.

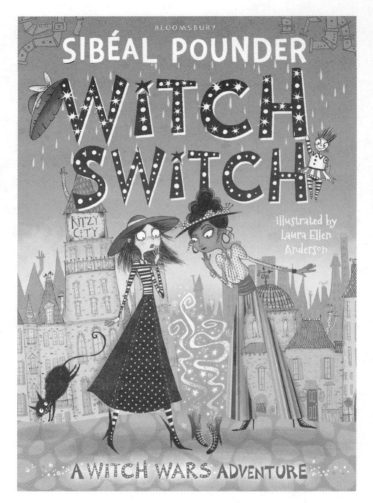

Read on for a peek at
the next WITCH WARS adventure

AVAILABLE NOW!

# The Cauldron Islands

'I HATE it here!' Fluffanora roared, kicking her foot and sending an extremely sparkly shoe sailing across the room.

'Frogs,' Tiga groaned, as it hit her square in the face.

They had been on the Cauldron Islands for two whole weeks and Fluffanora had been flinging shoes since they arrived.

The Cauldron Islands were where the Brews spent their summers. It had once been home to all the cauldron factories, but since witches had stopped using cauldrons, except perhaps for storing shoes or hitting burglars with, the factories had closed down. Mrs Brew had bought the largest cauldron factory, Crinkle Cauldrons – they were the best cauldrons and you could

tell them apart from other cauldrons because they had crinkly looking handles. A lot of witches had complained that the crinkle in the cauldron made it impossible to hold and so many spilled their potions and burnt their feet, but Tina Gloop, the owner of Crinkle Cauldrons, said they obviously just had wonky hands.

When Crinkle Cauldrons had closed down, Mrs Brew had converted the factory into a huge summerhouse. A bunch of other Ritzy City witches read about it in *Toad* magazine and copied her, and the neighbouring islands were also revamped. The murky waters were cleaned up and Bubble Beach, owned by Berta Bubble, was soon peppered with holiday houses and fun little clubs, including the two most popular ones, the Hubble Hut, popular with the Brews and other witches from Ritzy City, and the Toil & Trouble Tavern, which was frequented by evil witches and the Pearl Peak families.

Tiga and Fluffanora had peeked into the Toil & Trouble Tavern on the first day they arrived and spotted a bunch of witches twirling around in the middle of the room to a really evil song called 'I Want To Curse Your

Loved Ones' by the Silver Rats, a weird band Fluffanora described as 'complete slime'. Apparently they were Aggie Hoof's absolute favourite band. Fluffanora had shown Tiga a picture – there were three of them, all dressed in tutus with chunky black boots, and they had little rat ears poking out of the tops of their hats and their faces were painted silver.

The Hubble Hut was much better, and it served Clutterbucks drinks.

'Tiga, is your head all right?' Mrs Brew cried as she raced over to her.

'I've accidentally hit her with seven shoes in the last two days,' Fluffanora began.

'*Nine*,' Tiga said through gritted teeth.

Fluffanora shrugged. 'She's *fine*. She has a strong head.'

'Fluffanora,' Mrs Brew snapped, 'you have been behaving terribly.'

'Well then, let me go back to Ritzy!' Fluffanora shouted back.

It was well known throughout Sinkville that Fluffanora was not a fan of the Cauldron Islands. Everyone knew this because *Toad* magazine had once featured an article called 'Fluffanora Is Not a Fan of the Cauldron Islands'. It had described Fluffanora's various attempts over the years to escape holidays there. There was the time she had 10,000 cats delivered to Bubble Beach and ran around screaming, 'Oh no, the PLAGUE OF CATS! RUN, SAVE YOURSELVES!' Or the time she paid the old witch with the cart of disgusting hats to walk up and down the beach shouting, 'GENUINE HATS WHAT GOT STUCK IN THE PIPES! GENUINE HATS WOTS GOT STUCK IN THE PIPES!' to annoy everyone. Fluffanora had even attempted to make cauldrons cool again, hoping that if cauldrons were in demand, they would need the Cauldron Islands' factories back.

None of her attempts worked. Especially not that cat one. Most witches would welcome a plague of cats. They can't get enough of them.

Unlike Fluffanora, Tiga *loved* the Cauldron Islands. There was so much fun stuff to do – like wartling (almost the same as snorkelling, only instead of a snorkel and mask you magic giant warts to cover your whole face, so you can breath under water). Tiga spent hours exploring the cool caves and underwater walkways below Bubble Beach. The weird thing was, there wasn't a single fish, just lots of frogs dressed in different outfits – there was one in a stripy dress, and one wearing a small box hat. She did spot one frog *dressed* as a fish, sitting on a rock, sipping out of a shell cup next to a frog dressed as a mermaid.

Mrs Brew had explained to Tiga that you would never find a fish near the Cauldron Islands. They had decided to swim away to the north of Sinkville, around the cove area, because they found the frogs insufferable.

'*PLEASE*, can we go home? I want to go to Clutterbucks,' Fluffanora begged.

Mrs Brew shook her head. 'You can drink Clutterbucks at the Hubble Hut. You need a better reason than that to go back.'

Little did the three of them know, sitting in the cauldron-shaped post box outside was a letter containing a very, *very* good reason to go back …

# Fran in a Caravan

Fran was the first one to notice Peggy was missing.

She had been stopping by at Linden House to 'help' (boss about) Peggy every day since she'd become Top Witch, suggesting changes like creating a huge statue of Fran, painting a gigantic mural on the front of Linden House (of Fran) and changing the name of the city to FRAN. However, there were two days when she hadn't visited Peggy – and it was during that time that Peggy had VANISHED.

It had been a particularly windy couple of days in Sinkville and Fran's caravan, which hung precariously from a tree in Brollywood, had proved impossible to get out of – every time she pushed the door open the wind blew it shut again.

She had tried 9,846 times to get out.

She had even tried squeezing out of the tiny window, but her big beehive of hair wouldn't fit.

'HELP! I'M STUCK IN MY CARAVAN, MY ADORING FANS! GET ME OUT!' she cried, but no one heard. Apart from perhaps Julie, who flew past a few times.

'Is that you, Julie Jumbo Wings?! JULIE JUMBO WINGS?!'

Julie had simply held her head high and carried on flying.

According to her, she heard nothing.

When the wind eventually died down, Fran emerged from the caravan, her hair all lopsided and her dress curled up in the corners like a disgruntled flower. She blew the piece of hair dangling in her face and shot off towards Linden House.

She zoomed high over the Docks, which Peggy had got straight to work on when she had been crowned Top Witch. The Docks, where Peggy came from, had been a bit grubby but she soon fixed up lots of the houses – repairing wobbly floors and sewing holey curtains. And for the witches whose houses were beyond repair, Peggy had convinced Mrs Brew to donate beautiful shoes, and then she had done the shoe spell, which many witches all over Sinkville had watched her do during Witch Wars ('Little laces and heels in a heap, make me a better place to sleep!').

As well as making some very nice shoe-shaped houses, Peggy had sat outside Linden House on the first day of her reign and asked witches to tell her what they needed help with and what they would like to see changed. She had helped lots of witches. Old Hilda Trip had asked for new legs because hers were very old and hurt when she walked too far. Peggy couldn't really do anything about that, but she did make a very excellent flying armchair for Old Hilda. And a young witch called Alice Spoon said she'd really love to be a baker, but she didn't know where to start, so Peggy got her an apprenticeship at Cakes, Pies and That's About It, Really, the baker's. Fran had asked for a National Fran Day. Peggy said she would think about it.

'Peggy!' Fran cried as she flew towards the window Peggy always left open for her, 'I have been in the greatest of peril! I was stuck in my caravan for two days! With no access to my hairdresser!'

She sped up, 'Pegg–'

*THUD!*

The window was closed!

*Squeak*

*Squeak*

*Squeeeeak*

… went Fran, as she slid all the way down to the pavement, where she finally plopped into a little heap.

She barely had time to be furious about the fact Peggy had closed the window when the door to Linden House flew open.

Fran raised a finger, ready to give Peggy a good telling-off. But all she did was gasp.

There, standing proud in all her evil glory, was none other than Felicity Bat. And next to her was her smug sidekick, Aggie Hoof.

# A Far From Fabulous Note

'What does it say?' Fluffanora asked, eagerly peering over Tiga's shoulder at the note she had pulled from the cauldron-shaped post box.

Tiga shook her head in disbelief and read it out loud.

*Dearest Tiga,*
*My hair is A MESS, my wing is slightly crushed, and there is also a third thing that is ALMOST as terrible as those things that I must tell you.*

'She's run out of glittery dust, hasn't she?' Fluffanora said, rolling her eyes.

Tiga carried on.

*I can't find Peggy. Not only can I not find her but Felicity Bat has taken over Linden House! She and Aggie Hoof said Peggy left and put them in charge. Apparently she left them a note saying she was 'going away with the fairies'.*

*I immediately knew this was ridiculous nonsense. Why? Because the fairies are all far too busy to go away anywhere. Most of them are working on Crispy's new horror film TOE PINCHERS, apart from Donna, who is just being lazy. And there is Julie Jumbo Wings ... but Peggy wouldn't go anywhere with her. And anyway, she definitely flew past my caravan yesterday and ignored my cries for help.*

*I'm not sure what to do.*

*COME BACK TO RITZY CITY.*

*(Please also find enclosed a signed photo of my face.)*

*Thank you.*

*Your Very Fabulous Fairy,*

*Fran*

# Read the whole ritzy, glitzy, witchy series!